A Candlelight Ecstasy Romance®

**"YOU KNOW THERE'S SOMETHING
WONDERFUL BETWEEN US," HE MURMURED.**

"I stayed away from you for a whole week to find out if
what I felt for you was real and lasting. It is!" His mouth
closed over hers as he kissed her gently. Her mouth trembled. "You see how it is with us?"

"No. I don't see that at all." She tried to twist away
from him.

"Yes, you do. You're fighting it. You've totally disrupted my life and you're not going to scamper out of it
like a pup with your tail between your legs until I'm sure
it's what we both want."

"You have nothing to say about what I do! Now, bug
off! You're nothing to me, and . . . I despise everything
about you . . . especially that beard!"

His bright-green eyes mocked her. "You're a liar,
Glory, Glory," he drawled softly. "Not a word of what
you've said is true, and you know it."

CANDLELIGHT ECSTASY CLASSIC ROMANCES

THE TAWNY GOLD MAN, *Amii Lorin*
GENTLE PIRATE, *Jayne Castle*

CANDLELIGHT ECSTASY ROMANCES®

QUANTITY SALES

Most Dell Books are available at special quantity discounts when purchased in bulk by corporations, organizations, and special-interest groups. Custom imprinting or excerpting can also be done to fit special needs. For details write: Dell Publishing Co., Inc., 1 Dag Hammarskjold Plaza, New York, NY 10017, Attn.: Special Sales Dept., or phone: (212) 605-3319.

INDIVIDUAL SALES

Are there any Dell Books you want but cannot find in your local stores? If so, you can order them directly from us. You can get any Dell book in print. Simply include the book's title, author, and ISBN number, if you have it, along with a check or money order (no cash can be accepted) for the full retail price plus 75¢ per copy to cover shipping and handling. Mail to: Dell Readers Service, Dept. FM, P.O. Box 1000, Pine Brook, NJ 07058.

SHE WANTED RED VELVET

Dorothy Phillips

A CANDLELIGHT ECSTASY ROMANCE®

Published by
Dell Publishing Co., Inc.
1 Dag Hammarskjold Plaza
New York, New York 10017

Dell ® TM 681510, Dell Publishing Co., Inc.

Candlelight Ecstasy Romance®, 1,203,540, is a registered trademark of Dell Publishing Co., Inc., New York, New York.

ISBN: 0-440-18213-1

Printed in the United States of America

September 1986

10 9 8 7 6 5 4 3 2 1

WFH

To special people—
my cousins,
Norma and Ken Slane—
with special love.

To Our Readers:

We have been delighted with your enthusiastic response to Candlelight Ecstasy Romances®, and we thank you for the interest you have shown in this exciting series.

In the upcoming months we will continue to present the distinctive sensuous love stories you have come to expect only from Ecstasy. We look forward to bringing you many more books from your favorite authors and also the very finest work from new authors of contemporary romantic fiction.

As always, we are striving to present the unique, absorbing love stories that you enjoy most—books that are more than ordinary romance. Your suggestions and comments are always welcome. Please write to us at the address below.

Sincerely,

The Editors
Candlelight Romances
1 Dag Hammarskjold Plaza
New York, New York 10017

SHE WANTED RED VELVET

FOR MY READERS:

Gloria's Yummy Cake

1 package chocolate
cake mix
3/4 cup butter or
margarine
1/2 cup evaporated milk
1 16-oz. package
caramels

1 cup chocolate chips
1 cup nut meats
Optional: 1 cup coconut
Whipped cream

1. Preheat oven to 350° F.

2. Prepare chocolate cake batter according to directions on package. Bake 2/3 of the batter in a 9×13 pan and let cool.

3. In a double boiler melt together butter or margarine, milk, and caramels. Allow to cool and spread on cake.

4. Sprinkle chocolate chips and nut meats on top of cake. Coconut may be used instead of chocolate chips and nuts.

5. Dribble the remainder of the batter on top and bake for 15 minutes.

6. Allow to cool and serve with whipped cream.

CHAPTER ONE

It was late afternoon. The sun made patterns of speckled brightness on the leaf-strewn ground where it filtered through the trees surrounding the clearing beside the highway. The slim blond woman closed the door to the primitive outhouse, grabbed the hand of the four-year-old boy, and urged him along the path to the parking area.

"Why are we hurryin', Mom?"

"Come on, Peter. I'll tell you later." The woman took short running steps so the boy could keep up with her. When they reached the compact car, she quickly unlocked the door.

"Mom—"

"Get in the car," she commanded sharply with a glance back over her shoulder. She crowded into the bucket seat beside her son, locked the door, and reached over to make sure the door on the driver's side was locked.

"What are you scared of, Mom? You're scared, aren't ya? Is it them? What'd they say?" Peter pressed his nose against the window and stared at the two men coming down the graveled path from the building set back in the woods.

"I'm not scared, Peter," she said with far more confidence than she felt. *Dammit!* she thought. *If the car hadn't overheated, we wouldn't be sitting in this deserted rest area; we would practically be at Aunt Ethel's by now.*

"I'm hot. Can I roll down the window?"

"No," she said sharply, then moaned silently to herself. Why didn't I think to put the hood down before we got in the car? Aloud she said, "As soon as they leave, we'll go."

"They've got big motorcycles, and pictures on their arms. They're funny."

"Crawl into the backseat, honey. Come on, I'll help you."

She boosted the child into a small space next to pillows, toys, blankets, a small overnight case, and a cardboard box containing a whining puppy. She looked out the window and wondered if she'd be able to back out of the circular drive with the U-Haul trailer attached to the car. All the way out from Cincinnati she had been careful to keep out of a situation that would require backing the car for any distance.

The men were standing in front of the car, now, out of sight behind the raised hood.

"Cisco's crying. He's got to pee-pee."

"He'll have to wait."

"Mom—he don't want to wait. He's got to go—bad."

"Shhh . . ." She scarcely heard what Peter said. The uneasiness that had flooded her the moment she came out of the rest room with her small son and saw the two huge motorcycles parked in front of her car, and the men who then stepped from around the end of

12

the men's building, now escalated into full-fledged fear.

They had passed her fifty miles back down the highway, slowed down to twenty miles an hour, and weaved back and forth in front of her for several miles. She had honked the horn and tried to get away from them, to no avail; then, suddenly, they had let her go, when they spotted a highway patrol car parked on an overpass ahead. She had increased her speed to get as far ahead of them as possible, and had put them out of her mind when she could no longer see them in the rearview mirror.

This part of Montana was sparsely populated, and the small towns were far apart; at times she and Peter would go for miles and miles without meeting a car. In Lewistown she had pulled into a service station and filled her gas tank to be sure she would have enough fuel to get to her Aunt Ethel's motel and trailer park.

Soon after Lewistown the state highway had begun winding around the foothills and climbing into the rugged mountainous region. The small car that had brought them so far without so much as a cough from the engine had started to send distress signals in the form of a flashing red light on the dashboard. She had been so relieved to see the rest area, because by this time Peter was complaining he had to "go."

Now Gloria wished fervently she had taken a chance on the car's making the top of the hill; she could have coasted on the way down the other side and cooled the motor. In the middle of checking the engine she had stopped to take Peter to the bathroom. As a result the stupid hood was up. She couldn't drive away, and she couldn't see what the men were doing in front of her.

Suddenly the hood came down, and a whiskered face grinned at her. The hood was lifted, then lowered, in rapid succession.

"Peekaboo, pretty woman."

Oh, dear God! What will they do? The words never came out of her mouth; she didn't want to frighten Peter. She turned the key in the ignition, started the motor, and put the car in reverse, praying she would be able to back the car and trailer around the curve and onto the highway. The motor stopped. Damn! She turned the switch and pumped the accelerator. Nothing!

"What's the matter, Mom?"

"Be still, Peter . . . please—" Panic began to take hold, and she turned the key again and again. Grrrr . . . Grrrr . . . "Please start! Oh, start, damn you!"

The hood was slammed down so hard the car shook. "Doggy! Looky here what we found." The man with a sleeveless shirt and brass armbands yelled triumphantly and waved several long wires in front of the windshield.

"Go away and leave us alone!" Gloria yelled. The fear that rose in her throat almost choked her. They had taken some wires out of her engine; now she and Peter were really trapped.

"C'mon out an' play, pretty thin'. Ain't ya hot in there with them windows rolled up?"

One of the men sprang up onto the hood of the car and jumped up and down. He had long, frizzy hair and a leather thong tied about this forehead. The thin metal crackled and protested, and finally gave way under the weight of the heavy man.

Peter began to cry. "Mom! What're they doin'? I'm scared!"

"They can't get in the car, honey. Someone will be along soon and they'll go away. Then we'll go on to Aunt Ethel's." She made a great effort to speak calmly. *If anyone does come along,* she thought, *it's doubtful they'll turn in while those two despicable creatures are in sight.* "We'll just sit here and not look at them— Hey, stop that!" Gloria yelled. They were rocking the car, now, so violently that her head banged against the window.

"Who-eee! Ain't she a hot mama chick? Here, chicky, chick, chick—"

"Make 'em stop, Mom!"

The roar of a motor coming into the rest area caused her to turn hopefully, but hope turned to panic when she saw another large, black motorcycle come past the trailer and pull up ahead of the car. The rider wore boots, jeans, a sleeveless shirt, and a bright-blue helmet with a visor. He sat for a moment watching the two men rock the car before he leisurely got off the cycle and stood beside it.

"Whatta you got here?"

"What's it to ya?"

"Not friendly, huh?"

"If'n ya mean are we sharin', we ain't." The man on the hood jumped onto the top of the car, and the roof crackled and groaned beneath his weight.

"I know most of the cycle boys around here. Where're you from?" The newcomer stood leaning against his machine with his arms folded over his chest.

"We're from Chicago, man. From the Big Windy. What's your play? You figurin' to move in?"

"Maybe."

The man on the top of the car jumped to the ground. The two hoodlums moved to the front and stood shoulder to shoulder against the man in the blue helmet.

"Ya gonna do it all by yourself?" The frizzy-haired man took a step away from his friend.

The big shoulders lifted in a careless shrug. "Do you see anyone else?"

"Back off while ya can, big man."

"I'll say the same to you."

"You got no brains a-tall," the frizzy-haired man said, then glanced toward his more heavily built companion.

"Maybe," the newcomer said again. "Ride out. Leave her alone. You've got no business hasslin' a woman with a kid."

"Ha! Ya hear that, Boomy? The country boy's tellin' us to ride out. He's got cow manure for brains if he thinks we'll ride out and leave the split for him. Didn't ya hear us say we're from the Big Windy, hayseed?"

"Yeah, I heard you. That makes you pretty tough, huh?" The man moved away from his motorcycle, his legs spread apart, his fists resting on his hipbones.

Gloria rolled down the window a few inches so she could hear what was being said.

"Tough enough," Boomy said boastfully. He spit in the dirt, and it landed dangerously close to the other man's feet. "I think I'll take me a little spin on that machine of his." He grinned at his friend.

"Don't try it," the man said quietly.

"Haw, haw, haw—we're goin' to have to teach him some manners."

Boomy took only two steps toward the cycle before the man in the helmet exploded into action. His hands and his feet seemed to lash out simultaneously, knocking Boomy off his feet and sending him into the dirt. The other man got a foot in the groin; he screamed and doubled up on the ground. Boomy rolled to his feet like a cat, started forward, then stopped. Holding his arms out to his side menacingly, he spread his feet and edged forward, waiting for his chance to attack.

"Don't do it, punk. I'm warning you, I can break your neck." The voice from behind the visored helmet cautioned, "Get on your machine and clear out while you're in one piece."

"Who in the hell's going to help you, country boy? I'll bust head, man. We was here first."

"Okay. If you want to ride out of here with some broken bones, c'mon and get it."

The hoodlum sprang; the other man grabbed his arm, twisted it, and threw him over his shoulder. Boomy fell out of sight in front of the car. Gloria heard a screech of pain and held her breath; Peter's arms were wound so tight about her neck she could scarcely breathe anyway. The man in the helmet stood calmly looking down at the man on the ground. Boomy got slowly to his feet, holding his elbow.

"Ya broke my arm!" he accused, his voice quivering. His face was deathly white.

"I told you what you'd get, but you wouldn't listen.

17

You're lucky I didn't break your neck. Now, get the hell outta here and take this jerk with you before I break your leg too."

"I can't ride," he whined, holding his arm close to his chest.

"Ride or walk. It makes no difference to me. Go on back to Chicago and crawl into your hole. You're not fit to be among decent people." The man's broad back was to Gloria. He stood by while the men mounted their cycles and rode slowly out of the rest area. He followed a short distance and watched them go down the highway.

It was stifling hot inside the car. Gloria rolled the window down a few more inches and held Peter's face to the breeze. The child sniffled, the puppy yelped. Gloria watched the man cautiously. He unfastened the chin strap on his helmet, lifted it from his head, and placed it on the seat of his motorcycle before he turned toward the car.

Gloria sucked in her breath and quickly rolled up the window. The man had thick, curly black hair and a full black beard; the only part of his face she could see were his eyes, beneath heavy black brows. His shirt was open to the waist, and his chest was covered with dark hair. He was big, broad shouldered, and had heavily muscled arms and a thick neck. She looked into light greenish-gray eyes. *Oh, Lord! At least there's only one of him,* she thought fearfully.

"Aren't you about to burn up in there?"

Gloria shook her head.

"You must be." Peter began to cry again. "Look, lady, I'm not going to hurt you. Open the window before the kid has heat stroke."

"Go away."

"Okay." He went to his cycle and leaned against it with his arms crossed over his chest.

Gloria waited, hoping he would ride away. When he continued to stand there, she rolled down the window, watching him carefully to see if he might make a sudden move toward the car. Peter lifted his face to the cool breeze.

"Is he goin' to hurt our car, Mom?"

"I don't know, honey. We've got to wait—"

"Can't we go? You said we was almost to Aunt Ethel's."

"We are, but the other men pulled some wires out of our car and it won't start."

"Why'd they do that?"

"I don't know. They were bad men."

"Is he bad too?"

"I . . . don't know—"

"I'm no saint, boy. But I don't hurt women and kids." The man flashed a smile that was almost lost behind the beard. The only way Gloria knew it was there was by the crinkles at the corners of his eyes.

She rolled the glass down partway. Peter stuck his head out the window, but she tried to pull him back.

"I'd a beat 'em up, if I was big."

"Yeah? Well, I did it for you, this time. You can pay me back someday."

"My dog's got to potty."

"Peter! Hush up!"

"Let him out and I'll watch him."

"No! Peter—"

"Lady, I can understand your being nervous and scared. Those jerks were for real. But I sent 'em packin', didn't I? Look, I've not attacked a woman with a kid for a whole week now."

She ignored his attempt to be funny. "How do I know you won't harm us?"

" 'Cause I'm tellin' you. Are you going to sit there on your butt all night?"

"My car won't start."

"I know that. I can see the wires hanging out."

"Why did you stop?"

"I saw you at the station back in Lewistown and knew you and the kid were alone."

"You were following me!"

"I was going home. Where are you going, anyway? And what in hell are you doing out on the highway dressed like that?"

Gloria's mouth dropped open and a tingling warmth flooded her face that had nothing to do with the heat in the car. She glanced quickly down at the brief tan shorts and the backless halter she was wearing.

"There's no air conditioning in this car, not that it's any business of yours."

"You're asking for trouble going around half naked," he insisted. "Half of Lewistown was gawking at you."

"Cisco wants out." Peter was holding the squirming puppy.

The man came to the car. "Hand me the pup, boy."

"Will ya hurt him, mister?"

"Naw. I like dogs."

Without hesitation Peter passed the puppy through the opening and watched anxiously as the big hands took him. "His name's Cisco," he called. "What's yours?"

"Jack. Here, now, little fellow. . . ." He held the small brown body close to his chest and rubbed between the furry ears with long, strong fingers before he gently set him on the ground. The puppy scurried about in the grass and Peter craned his neck to watch him. The man looked directly at Gloria. "Have you decided what you're going to do?"

"Not . . . yet."

"We're goin' to Aunt Ethel's and we're almost there," Peter said, no longer shy and afraid.

"Where's that?"

"My aunt has a motel west of here."

"The Rusty Cove? I pass it on my way home. It's about ten miles from here."

"Will you stop there and tell my aunt where we are and ask her to send someone for us?"

"I could do that, but it'll be night long before they come back for you. Do you want to sit here in the dark?"

"I don't *want* to," Gloria said crossly. "I don't have much choice."

"Yes, you do. Lock up the car. I'll take you and the boy to the motel on my cycle. They've got a pickup and I'll bring it back and tow your car in."

"We can't ride on . . . that *thing!*" The idea was out of the question. Ride with him? For all she knew he was cut from the same cloth as the men who had wrecked her car. He certainly looked just like them.

"Cisco! Come back—" Peter opened the door on the passenger side and darted after the puppy, who was running toward the highway.

21

"Peter!" Gloria yelled frantically.

Jack ran after the puppy and scooped him up before he reached the road. He came back and knelt down beside Peter.

"How long have you had him?"

"We got him in Des Moines. He was in a store window by the motel. He was cryin' and wantin' out. Mom said I'd could have him if I learned how to take care of him. She said Aunt Ethel lived in the country and she wouldn't mind. Mom said I could name him what I wanted to, so I named him Cisco like the man on TV. He's the good guy."

"Is the Cisco Kid still on? I used to watch him when I was a kid."

"Peter," Gloria called sharply. "Get back in the car." She stood beside the open door, her heart hammering with fear, her shapely bare legs trembling. Sweat plastered her short blond hair to her forehead and pale cheeks.

Peter and the man came back to the car. His height topped Gloria's five-foot-seven-inch frame by more than a half a foot. He was broad in the shoulders and chest, yet solid and lean through the waist and hips. His clothes were clean, but his hair was too long and his boots were old and scuffed. She wished he didn't have that damned beard so she could see his face.

Gloria stood still, her head tilted back and a big flashlight clinched in her fist like a weapon. She reached out and grabbed Peter's arm and pulled him close to her. The green eyes glinted as the man assessed her stance. Suddenly he laughed. It was a pleasant laugh, full of amusement.

"You've got more guts than brains, sister. Didn't

you see me break that punk's arm? I could have just as easily broken his leg or his stupid neck. You wouldn't stand a chance against me with that flashlight, but I admire your courage. A mother protecting her cub—"

"What . . . are you going to do?"

"Nothin', dammit! If I didn't have this beard and wasn't riding a motorcycle you'd be glad to accept my help. Isn't that true? You're a redneck, sister! You don't like what you see. Well, that's too damn bad. I don't like what I see either." He paused, and when she didn't say anything, he continued, slowly and patiently, "I don't hassle women with kids and I don't really like being on my cycle in these mountains at night, so if you're coming with me, let's get going."

"You can't take both of us . . . and the puppy. We can't leave him here."

"Of course not. The boy can sit in front of me, you can sit behind."

"I've never ridden—"

"There's nothing to it."

"Let's go, Mom. I'll hold Cisco. I want to ride on the motorcycle. *Var . . . oom! Var . . . oom!*"

"Hush up, Peter," Gloria said impatiently. "I . . . want to see some identification."

"Oh, for God's sake! What difference would that make? I could show you anything, and you'd know no more about me than you do now. Believe me, I don't have designs on your *body,* lady. It's nice enough, but kinda skinny for my taste. Besides I'd have to be a pervert to take you with the hotshot looking on."

"Watch your mouth," she warned, glancing at her son.

"Mom's name's Gloria. Mine's Peter. Yours is Jack.

I know a girl in Cincinnati named Jackie. I don't like 'er."

"Get your purse and lock the car."

"But—"

"Lady!"

"Her name's Gloria."

"Okay, okay. C'mon, Glory." He chuckled, reached for his helmet, and put it down over Peter's head. "You'll have to wear this, big shot. It's too big, but it's better than nothin'."

Peter was delighted. "Look at me, Mom."

The man's thoughtful gesture finally convinced her to go with him. She reached inside the car for her bag and swung it over her shoulder.

"Does the boy have a jacket he can zip or button up? That way he can carry the pup." The man's voice was close to her ear, and she froze. Sensing her tension he backed away and laughed softly. "You're about to go up with the shades, Glory. Have a little faith. Jesus had a beard too."

"Don't be sacrilegious," she snapped.

Gloria rummaged among the blankets and found the jacket, then locked the car. Peter asked if he looked like a spaceman in the helmet.

"Just like an astronaut," she said lightly, helping him into the jacket.

"Cisco'll have to ride in here, sport. Do you think you can keep him still?" The man knelt beside Peter, slipped Cisco inside the jacket, and zipped it up to make a deep pocket.

"Sure. He likes me better'n anybody."

"Okay. Let's go." He straddled the machine and balanced it with a foot planted on each side. He lifted

Peter up and set him in front of him. "Hop on." He looked at Gloria over his shoulder, and his eyes traveled from hers to the V of the halter and on down to the bare midriff.

"I . . . where do I sit?" Now she was painfully aware of her abbreviated costume. She hadn't given it a thought until he'd mentioned it.

"Straddle the seat. You didn't expect to ride sidesaddle, did you?" At the hint of amusement in his voice her wide, generous mouth tightened, and her chin lifted defiantly. She looked back at him with cold dislike in her amber eyes, swung her leg over, and sat down.

"Put your feet here." He reached back and grasped the calf of her bare leg and guided her foot to the place behind his. "Hold on to my belt. I doubt if you're too anxious to put your arms around me," he said with a chuckle, and pushed down on the lever that started the machine.

"Hold on, Peter," she yelled over the roar. *Oh, Christ and all that's holy! What in the world are we doing on this thing?*

"Don't worry about him." The words came from the bearded face.

Don't worry! How can I help it, for goodness' sake? The machine bumped over the uneven ground and up onto the smooth highway. There was not a car in sight, and as the cycle picked up speed, Gloria's arms inched around the man's waist, and her hands grabbed hold of her son's jacket. *Oh, baby! What have I gotten you into?*

The breeze was cool on her damp skin, and soon she was shivering and hovering close to the broad back in front of her. Her short blond hair, with its simple, stylish cut, was swept back by the wind. After the first few minutes she had to admit that he *wasn't* going terribly fast and that he *was* being careful. They reached the top of a long incline and started down.

Gloria relaxed a little. *Oh, Marvin, if you could see me now!* A small giggle escaped her lips. He would be horrified at the thought of his wife, his ex-wife, on a motorcycle with a bearded giant who looked as if he were a member of the Hell's Angels. Unbending, fastidious, status-conscious Marvin, who was humiliated when his wife stooped to help a servant clean up a spilled drink, but who thought nothing of maneuvering a small businessman out of his holdings in order to add them to his conglomerate, would see nothing at all amusing about her and Peter on the motorcycle. As a matter of fact he was more than likely going through Cincinnati with a fine-tooth comb looking for them.

There were times when Gloria was completely mystified by Marvin's attitude toward her. They had been divorced for a year, yet he still thought he could control her life. He detested Peter and had told her, time and again, that he fervently regretted the day they had adopted him.

How foolish she had been to think she wanted red velvet. She gave herself a few minutes to remember how it had been in those days. She had lived all her life in a small town in southern Ohio. Her mother and father, and her older brothers and sisters, had always worked in the local bakery, and they were determined she would seek employment there too. But, equally determined not to be trapped in a dead-end situation, she went to Cincinnati to work for a company who collected rating statistics for everything from television programs to politics. Every day, eight hours a day, five days a week, she had sat at a machine and punched in numbers for a salary that barely covered car payments, rent, and food. The work was boring, but the city offered many cultural activities lacking in the small town.

It was at Christmastime, just a few days before the company dance, when she saw the red velvet dress in the store window. The rich red material symbolized everything she had ever dreamed of having, and she wanted that dress more than she had ever wanted anything in her life. It had been totally out of character for her to withdraw all her savings and buy the dress, but she did. When she wore it to the dance she felt like a princess. And in it she attracted one of Cincinnati's wealthiest men, Marvin Eugene Masterson, the owner of the company she worked for, and her life was drastically changed forever.

I wanted red velvet, she mused. *But I soon discovered that red velvet doesn't wear well day after day. After a while it looks tawdry and cheap, just as Marvin's values were tawdry and cheap, false and insincere, when the glamorous facing was torn away.*

Thank God, she murmured against the stranger's back, *Peter and I have finally gotten away from Cincinnati. This is a new beginning for us. I'll work hard and teach my son respect for himself and for others and that the world doesn't begin and end with a bank account or prestigious friends.*

Now, if only we get to Aunt Ethel's—if only I haven't made another serious mistake in judging a man's character. . . .

CHAPTER TWO

Gloria was too cold to notice that the mountain road wound through a densely wooded area, and that they had not passed a single dwelling since leaving the rest area. Her arms circled the man in front of her and her hands clutched her son's jacket. The minute the sun finished its daily journey across the sky and was out of sight behind the mountains, the air turned cold. Shivering, she hugged the man's back; goose bumps stood out on her arms and legs, and she clenched her jaws to keep her teeth from chattering. She was too numb to realize that the chilly air had made her nipples rock hard, and that only two thin layers of material lay between them and the skin on the man's back.

Jack Evans was more than aware of the small, skimpily dressed woman who clung to his back, the nipples that pressed against him, and the arms about his waist. He felt a sudden, deep hunger for the soft warmth and companionship, the sweetness, of a woman, and the love and trust of a child. He squinted into the wind and dredged from his mind all the reasons for suppressing that longing. *Hell, Evans,* he said to himself, *get her and the kid on down to Ethel's and flag your butt on home. You're free as the breeze. If you let yourself get involved with this kind of woman, the first thing you know she'll be wanting you to get a nine-to-five job, a briefcase, a house, a station wagon, a three-piece suit . . .*

They rounded a deep bend in the road and turned onto a graveled drive, bumped over a span of metal that covered the deep drainage ditch that ran alongside the highway, and passed beneath the orange-lettered sign: RUSTIC COVE. They stopped in front of the long, narrow brown building surrounded by a thick stand of trees. The doors along the length of the motel were bright orange.

Gloria was too stiff and cold to move. Jack loosened her hold on Peter's jacket so he could lift the boy off the machine. She stirred when the warmth of his body left hers and looked at him dully. Her short hair was a tangled mess, her nose red as a cherry, and her lips blue. He placed two large hands around her waist and lifted her up and off the cycle as he had done with Peter. He held her for the space of a couple of breaths until her legs could hold her.

"Are you all right?"

"Noooo—I'll ne-ver be all ri-ght again." Was the clicking sound she heard her teeth chattering? It was no wonder she couldn't talk.

"If you'd have dressed decently you wouldn't be so cold," he said unfeelingly. "How about you, hotshot? Are you cold too?" He lifted the helmet off Peter's head and placed it on the seat of the cycle.

"Naw . . . that was *fun!* I'm goin' to get me a motorcycle when I grow up."

"Heaven forbid," Gloria muttered.

"Gloria! Is that you?" A short, plump woman in a

29

royal-blue jogging suit flung open the screen door. The metal sign, OFFICE, clanged when it slammed shut.

"What's left of me, Aunt Ethel."

"Land-a-Goshen'! What happened? What are you doin' with Jack? Oh, never mind, you're here, that's what matters. I thought you'd be bigger, but you ain't no bigger than when I saw you last. I figured you was about thirteen then." She talked in a steady stream as she wrapped her arms around Gloria. Her twinkling eyes looked down. "This is Peter? *Eeekkk . . .*" she squealed. "I thought you were a baby, but you're almost as big as your ma. Come give Aunt Ethel a kiss."

"I got a puppy," he announced as soon as he had kissed the smooth cheek. "See!" He pulled the squirming ball of brown fur out of the front of his jacket. "I think he's got to pee-pee. Do you like dogs? Can I put him down?"

"Oh, Peter," Gloria groaned.

"Course I like dogs. Land sakes! Put him down. You can't expect such a little fellow to hold it forever." She took the puppy and sat him down on a grassy patch beside the drive. "Watch that he don't go to the woods," she cautioned. Then, "Hi, Jack."

"Hello, Ethel. Is this the new help you were expecting?"

"Aunt Ethel, I'm freez-ing."

"Well, I should think so. What in the world were you doin' on that cycle? Where's your clothes? Where's your car? C'mon in. I'll swear, I wasn't lookin' for you to come ridin' in with Jack."

"Her car's down at the rest area, Ethel. Give me the keys to your pickup and I'll go pull it in."

"Way down there? Heavens! What's it doin' there?

No wonder you're cold, if'n you rode that cycle all the way up here."

"I . . . had car trouble. It's got a U-Haul hooked on be-hind it. Aunt Ethel, I don't think he can—"

"Is there anyone here who can go with me?" Jack asked, ignoring Gloria's protest and looking at Ethel.

"Gary's out back working on his rig; he'll go with you. C'mon in, Gloria. Ain't no sense you standing out here freezing. Jack'll take care of your car." Ethel opened the door and motioned her inside. Jack followed Ethel, looming over her five-foot figure; *He looks more than ever like a caveman,* Gloria thought.

"The keys are on the desk, Jack. When you and Gary get back, c'mon in for supper."

Gloria stood hugging herself, trying not to shiver. Her eyes went from her aunt to the black-bearded man and back again; her little gray-haired aunt seemed to be perfectly at ease with him. He walked across the room and then went outside without a word or a glance at her. She heard him say something to Peter, and she started for the door just as her son came in holding the puppy.

"We'll have to find a box and make him a bed, and teach him what he can do and what he can't," Ethel said. "We'll lay out some papers too. We don't want him to get in the habit of piddlin' on the floor."

"Oh, Aunt Ethel! I didn't realize how much trouble the dog would be." Gloria said apologetically.

"Ain't no trouble." Ethel's eyes sparkled vividly. "All boys ought'a have a dog to take care of. Why, Peter an' that pup'll liven this ol' place up considerably."

"No doubt," Gloria said with a worried frown. She

and Peter followed her into the living quarters behind the office. Ethel went through a door and was back almost instantly.

"Here. Put on this old bathrobe. Land sakes, didn't you know that just as soon as the sun goes down it gets colder than the bottom of a well out here?"

"I didn't, but I certainly do now." Gloria slipped into the worn flannel robe that was too short for her, and belted it tightly around her waist.

The room was small, but warm and cozy. An oval braided rug covered most of the floor. A couch with a freshly washed slipcover and pillows stood on one side of a cobblestone fireplace, and a rocking chair on the other. The walls were lined with paintings of Western scenes. Gloria moved over to peer at the one over the fireplace.

"Don't look too close," Ethel said with a merry laugh. "I'm one of those paint-by-number artists. I love doin' it, and it passes the time during the winter when things slow up around here."

"You're kidding," Gloria exclaimed. "They're beautiful."

"My, my." Ethel shook her head. "I just can't get over that you're here. And of all the times we've talked on the phone I pictured you as bigger than what you are; why, a good wind from the north would blow you clear to Mexico." She turned on a lamp beside the rocker. "Here, sit down and tell me about the trip. I swear, it was a shock to see you come ridin' in on that cycle with Jack. It's a good thing he come along, though. Traffic slows to almost nothin' in the late evenin'."

Gloria sat down and Peter came to lean against her

knee. "We had a good time driving out, didn't we, Peter? Our only problem was when we stopped at the rest area down the road. The car had started to heat up; I guess it was from pulling the trailer." She told her aunt about the two hoodlums, downplaying the seriousness of the encounter because Peter was listening with rapt attention.

"They stomped on our car, but Jack come and beat 'em up. He hit 'em." Peter put the dog in Gloria's lap and demonstrated as he talked. "He hit 'em to the ground and he said, 'Get the hell out—' "

"Peter! Watch what you're saying. Little boys don't use words like that."

"That's what Jack said. He said—"

"Never mind." The dog began to whine. Gloria lifted her eyes to the ceiling in a gesture of silent suffering.

Ethel laughed and pointed toward the swinging doors. "Honey, there's a clothes basket in that room behind the kitchen and a stack of old towels on the washer. Fix that pup a bed. He's tired and wants to sleep."

After Peter left, Ethel sank down on the couch. "He took to Jack, seems like."

"He's had so little male companionship that he takes to anyone who gives him a little attention. As I told you on the phone, Marvin's name is on his adoption papers, but he's never been a father figure. Peter doesn't even think of him as his father. He seldom speaks of him, and when he does he refers to him as 'he.' "

Ethel clicked her tongue against the roof of her mouth and shook her head sadly. "If that ain't the

33

limit! What's the world comin' to? Oh, well . . . you and Peter are here now. I never had a chick of my own. George and I just rammed around in the Oklahoma oil fields most all our married life. He loved workin' on the oil rigs; he did it until his hands were so crippled up with arthritis that he couldn't do it anymore. Then we sunk our nest egg in this here motel and campground. Two, three years after we come here he had his heart attack and was gone." She paused. "My, my, I miss him. Sometimes I get so low my tail's draggin' in the mud. Then I think of what George said a few days before he died: 'Ethel,' he said, 'if anythin' happens to me, you take the bit in yore teeth and stay right here. This here's a good place for you. The folks like you, and them truckers think yore a jim-dandy.' You know, George was right. Oh, I don't mean about the truckers likin' me, I mean that this is a good place for me. I've got a lot of friends that come and go and keep tabs on me, and I like doin' for 'em." Ethel's bright-blue eyes glinted and her round face broke into a smile. "Now, after all these years, I got me a family too."

"How come you and Dad never kept in touch with each other, Aunt Ethel?"

"George and I used to go back East once in a while. The last time we was back, you was just a young sprout. I think your mother kind of resented the affection me and Ernest had for each other, so . . ." Her voice trailed away. "How is Ernest?"

"He's fine. He retired from the bakery two years ago. Now he's working part time at a self-service gas station. He had so much time on his hands that he didn't know what to do with himself."

"I can understand it. If you got any gumption a-tall you'll keep on a doin' somethin', anythin', 'till you drop dead, else you'll wither on the vine. Well . . . did you burn your bridges behind you when you pulled up to come out here?"

"Yes, I did, Aunt Ethel. Maybe it was foolish. I should have come out and stayed awhile before we moved in on you lock, stock, and barrel. Peter and I may be too much for you."

"You and Peter won't be too much for me," Ethel said staunchly. "My worry is that being a city girl, you'll get tired of being stuck out here in the boonies. We're more than twenty miles from town. Sometimes, after a heavy snowfall, it's days before the highway gets plowed out."

"I won't mind that. I like to read and to sew, but I've told you that before." Gloria smiled warmly at her aunt. "During the last few years our talks on the phone helped me to keep my sanity. You always said things that made perfectly good sense. Aunt Ethel, I feel closer to you than I do to my mother, father, or any of my brothers and sisters." She frowned. "I never told them about any of my problems with Marvin. They thought I had made a good 'catch' and that I was crazy when I left him."

"Dear child, you only get one time around in this life, and it ain't all downhill in the shade. Just because you've made a mistake, God doesn't expect you to live with it and be miserable for the rest of your life. George always said, 'Do what you want to do as long as it don't hurt anybody else. It won't make any difference a hundred years from now, anyway.'" She bounded off the couch. "I'd better look at the casserole. And I might ought to add more lettuce to the salad. I hadn't planned on feeding Jack. He's a lot of man to fill up."

Gloria followed her to the kitchen. "Who is he, Aunt Ethel? I didn't want to tell you in front of Peter, but he flew into those two hoodlums like a whirlwind and sent one of them off with a broken arm."

Ethel chuckled. "He's Jack Evans. He lives up north of us four or five miles in an old ghost town. He's fixed himself up a little place up there. It takes a lot to get Jack riled, but when he is—watch out. He's all right, and he's no dummy."

"Maybe not," Gloria said dryly. "But he sure looks like one. I was just as scared of him as I was of the other two. Why would a man want to look like that?"

"Oh, you mean the beard?" she asked with a twinkle in her eye. "Maybe it keeps him warm in the winter."

"This isn't winter. And I didn't mean only the beard. I mean the long hair, the sleeveless shirt, the tattoo on his arm, and that stupid motorcycle. Right away I thought he was a member of the Hell's Angels gang."

Ethel shot her niece a look of amusement. "Jack's all right." She put on two oven mitts and lifted the large pan out of the oven. "While we were working the oil fields, I learned not to judge a man by what was on the outside. Some of those greasy, shaggy-headed ol' boys were just as sweet as could be, honest as the day is long, and would give you the shirt off their backs. Then, sometimes we'd run into a dressed-up dandy who was all pretty and smelled nice, and find out that he was so crooked he'd have to be screwed into the ground when he died." She lifted the foil off the pan and put it back in the oven. "I hope you like lasagna."

"Peter and I love it. Aunt Ethel—how many people do you usually cook dinner for?"

"All the way from four to eight. I got started giving them supper when George and I discovered that's why people didn't stop here. People's got to stop where they can eat. The truckers will give me a call on the CB and let me know that they'll be here. I have regulars that stop on their way out and on their way back. I get a few salesmen, and some tourists in the summer. A few backpackers and tenters come in once in a while."

"I'm so glad you asked us to come out. This is the perfect time, before we have to move on to find a place for Peter to go to school."

"There's a good community school only ten miles up the road. Ain't no reason to cut your stay short for that. The school bus will pick him up."

"*Only* ten miles! Oh, Aunt Ethel, he'll be five years old! I couldn't possibly put him on a bus to travel ten miles to school every day."

"Don't worry about it now." Ethel took a stack of plates from the cabinet and carried them to the long table at the end of the kitchen. "You've got a whole year before your chick has to go out to meet the world."

"Come look, Mom. Come look at the bed I made for Cisco." Peter came into the kitchen, rubbing his eyes with the back of his hand.

Gloria went to him. "You're tired, honey. I bet Aunt Ethel could find you a little something to eat so you can go to bed."

37

"I wanna wait till Jack comes back. I'm not tired, Mom. Honest."

"I want to show you your room before Jack gets back with your things." Ethel came and took his hand. "C'mon. We'll go back to the front office. I had a connecting door put in. You and your mom will be in unit one."

"Aunt Ethel! Are we taking up one of your paying units? I thought you had two bedrooms in your living quarters. We'll be using a unit you can rent out."

"Land sakes! Quit your frettin'. You need a place where you can spread your things out and make yourself at home. I've nine other units, and they're hardly ever full. If one of my regulars comes and we're full up, he can sleep on the couch."

She opened the door into a spacious room. There was a large double bed at one end with a rose-colored satin spread, and a twin bed at the other with a spread splashed with bright comic-book characters. Along one wall was a double chest, and in the corner a single. A warm beige carpet covered the floor. Ethel pranced in, turned on the light, and opened the door to the dressing room that also served as closet. Off this room was the bathroom.

Peter began to open the empty drawers and to play with the three-way lamp beside his bed.

"It isn't fancy," Ethel said lamely, as if she were seeing it through Gloria's eyes.

"It's perfect! I didn't expect to have so much room or a private bath. Oh, thank you, Aunt Ethel." She put her arms around the little woman and hugged her. "You've gone to so much trouble for us. I hope I'll be worth it to you."

Gloria was glad her aunt wasn't aware of the grandiose style she had lived in while married to Marvin. Even the high-rise she and Peter had moved into after the divorce was plush; Marvin owned the building, and in the settlement had insisted she was to live there with their son. In her desperation to leave him she had agreed. Marvin couldn't bear to lose control of anything, even a woman who didn't measure up to what he expected his wife to be. He had to have her under his thumb. Well . . . that was over now.

"Just having you and Peter here is all the thanks I want." Ethel was saying. "Now, let's shake a leg. I ring the supper gong at six-thirty. If Jack and Gary aren't here by then, we'll keep the food warm for them."

That proved to be unnecessary.

Gloria came to the table in an Indian-print caftan with a high neck and three-quarter-length sleeves. She and Peter took their places after Ethel had introduced them to an insurance adjuster, a bulk-paper salesman, an independent trucker, and to Gary, the man who had gone with Jack to get her car. He was a short, husky man who made no attempt to mask his curiosity. Bright, friendly eyes swept over her in frank appraisal, and she found herself returning his smile.

The meal was served family style; dishes were passed from left to right. Ethel kept up a merry line of chatter while she refilled the bread plate and poured coffee. The men teased her.

"Is this all we get?" Gary asked.

"You say that every time," Ethel shot back. "But I see you're not losing any weight."

Gloria was grateful that she wasn't expected to add much to the conversation. She placed tiny servings of food on Peter's plate and urged him to eat. He was so tired and sleepy he could barely keep his eyes open.

One time she lifted her head to find Jack's green eyes staring at her from across the table. Her large, tawny-gold eyes widened perceptibly and her lips suddenly felt dry. She was the first to look away. When she glanced back at him later, she was surprised to catch him studying her again. He really was a monolith of a man, she thought. His size alone was enough to intimidate without the hair and the beard. He seemed to be perfectly at ease, and ate enormous portions of food.

Gloria had caught the paper salesman eying him apprehensively and had to suppress a smile. She wondered what Jack would look like without all that hair on his face. The one thing she was sure of was that he was not young, for all his wild look. He was somewhere between thirty and forty, and she could detect a certain amount of polish beneath the rough exterior, when he chose to let it shine through.

Peter was half asleep by the time the meal was finished. His eyelids drooped and his legs were rubbery. Gloria stood, excused herself, and struggled to get him on his feet. For some time now he had been too heavy for her to carry.

"Come on, honey. Let's get you to bed." She shook him gently. He sagged against her. She took a few steps and he wrapped his arms about her legs. "Oh, honey, I know you're tired, but—"

"C'mon, hotshot. You're dead on your feet." Jack knelt down beside Peter and touched his shoulder. The child turned immediately, and his hands went up and about the man's neck. He was scooped up with one powerful arm.

"Where's . . . Cisco?" Peter mumbled.

"The pup's gone to bed. Don't you think that's where you should be?"

"Can I feel your whiskers, Jack?"

"Sure."

"They tickle."

"Yeah?" Gray-green eyes looked down into Gloria's. Surprised by the amusement that shone so blatantly, she flickered her eyelids in an instant of confusion. "Where to, ma'am?"

"Ah . . . this way." She went ahead of him to the office and through the door to their room. She flicked on the soft light beside Peter's bed and turned down the spread.

Jack laid the boy gently on the bed, lifted his small feet, slipped off his canvas shoes without untying them, and dropped them on the floor. He reached for the blanket and covered him.

"Are you goin' now, Jack?" Peter's eyes were only half open.

"Yeah, hotshot. I'm goin'."

"Will . . . you come back?"

"I don't know about that, kid. I've got things to do. You'd better get to sleep now."

"I want ya to come back—" Peter tried to sit up, but Jack held him down gently.

"We'll see, kid."

"That means no. *He* always said that. You're not ever comin' back." Peter's eyes filled with tears and his mouth trembled as if he was going to cry.

"Who said so? Well . . . okay, hotshot. I come by here once in a while. I'll stop in. How's that?"

"You're not just sayin' it?"

"Hey . . . I don't talk to hear my head rattle." Jack pretended to frown.

"Are you . . . sure? You're not just sayin' it?"

"Course, I'm not just sayin' it. If I say I'll be back, you can make book on it."

"What's that mean?"

"It means I'll see you the next time I come by. Good night, hotshot."

"Night, Jack. Night, Mom," Peter sang out happily. He snuggled contentedly under the blanket and was almost instantly asleep.

Gloria batted her lashes furiously to keep the tears at bay. She had had no idea of the depth of the child's disappointment concerning the man who was his legal father. Marvin's stock answer for everything Peter asked him had been "We'll see." Peter was right in saying it was the same as no.

"I should put on his pajamas," Gloria said, opening the suitcase.

"Why?"

"Well . . . because he always sleeps in pajamas."

"Why? Is there a law that says the kid's got to be roused up out of a good sleep to undress him so he can sleep? Doesn't make sense to me."

"I doubt if many of the things I do would make sense to you, Mr. Evans," she said carefully.

"Is that right?" He looked around the room. "Are you going to stay here?"

"I'm planning on it."

"You won't like it. You'll be bored," he said flatly.

"How do you know?" She felt a shiver of anticipation each time she looked at him. Anticipation of what? It was absurd that he was even here in her room.

"I know. You've run out here to escape from something. Is it being divorced?"

"What makes you so sure I'm divorced?"

He shrugged. "One out of every three women your age has been married at least once. There's no reason to believe you're any different."

"Thank you for the information, Mr. Gallup."

He ignored her sarcasm and glanced over to where Peter was sleeping, then down at her. His eyes narrowed. "Did your old man take his frustrations out on the kid?"

Gloria felt a tremor in her heart. "What makes you say that?"

"I'm not blind or deaf, Glory. The kid's hurtin' for masculine company. He's been disappointed a lot, hasn't he? Why didn't he say 'my dad'? Before I left with the pickup he told me that *he* didn't like puppies." He waited. "Well?" he insisted when she didn't say anything.

"It's none of your business."

"Yeah." He shrugged again and bent forward, and she imagined she felt his breath on her face. "You're right. It seems stupid to me that people get married in the first place. Stupider yet, when they have kids they don't want."

"For your information, Peter is wanted and loved. But I can understand why *you* would think the way you do about marriage. I'm sure it's too conventional for the likes of you."

He chuckled at her sarcasm, then he looked at her for so long a time that her self-confidence began to crumble. Critical eyes traveled over her trim body. She searched her mind for something cutting and clever to say that would put him firmly in his place. Why didn't he leave? Why was he still standing there? Her eyes held a definite shimmer of defiance when she met his glance. His eyes traveled over her face, taking in the wide amber eyes beneath arched brows, the straight nose, wide mouth, and the proud way her head lifted above her slender neck. Then he nodded his head, as if he had come to a decision about her.

There was something in his eyes, in the way they were assessing her, that made her breath quicken. She wasn't *afraid* of him, yet all her defenses were raised. She didn't fully understand this inner need to protect herself from him, it was just there and seemed to be purely instinctive. The chaos existed only in her mind, she was sure of that.

"Poor, scared little girl," he murmured, raising his hand to cup the back of her head. "You're almost as helpless as that kid over there." Then as if talking to himself, he said on a breath of a whisper, "Two little lambs being chased by the big, bad wolf."

"I'm neither poor, scared, nor chased, Mr. Evans." Gloria stepped back away from his hand, hoping her lie was convincing. She inhaled deeply, forcing herself to be calm; she desperately hoped that he didn't know how nervous she was. She moistened her dry lips. "Thank you for your help today. I'd like to pay you for going after my car."

"Okay. What are you offering?"

"Whatever you think it's worth," she said coolly. "I

won't quibble about the bill." It irritated and disappointed her that he was so willing to accept payment.

"Is that a promise?" he asked softly. His tone, more than his words, jarred her nerves. "On the surface you appear to be a typical example of a liberated woman, but underneath you're vulnerable, and scared to death. What in hell did that man do to you?"

She wanted to say something flip to let him know, in no uncertain terms, that the conversation was too personal and that she didn't appreciate his humor. But all she could manage was a look of disapproval, which did nothing but intensify the devilish look in his eyes.

"I'll write you a check, Mr. Evans," she stated curtly.

"I don't want your check, Mrs. Masterson."

"I'll pay you in cash."

"You said you wouldn't quibble about the price."

"I won't—"

"I want the boy for a day. I'll take him up to my place—"

"No!"

He was watching her, trying to read her face; her features were clouded by anger and confused emotions.

"I can see the wheels turning in her mind." He looked over her shoulder, as if he were talking to someone else. "She's thinking that I'm a pervert, a child molester, a ruthless criminal—"

"You could be . . . all those things," she said in a tight, breathless whisper.

"Instant analysis based on . . ."

"Based on . . . appearance!" Gloria's temper flared.

45

"Okay. Based on appearance. Your opinion of me would have been quite different if I had come into that rest area in a Buick station wagon, a Bill Blass suit, with a short haircut and a clean-shaven face. But remember the old saying, You can't tell a book by its cover."

"You said it, I didn't. I still appreciate what you did for us," she said with a proud lift of her head.

"Yeah, sure. Brawn comes in handy once in a while."

"Well . . . thank you, Mr. Evans, and . . . good night."

"You're quite welcome, Mrs. Masterson, and good night to you too." He placed one bent arm behind him and one in front and bowed deeply. "I really must be going. There's an orgy going on up at my place and a whole harem of naked women are waitin' to be pleasured by their favorite stud."

Gloria didn't allow a muscle in her face to move, although she felt his twinkling green eyes mocking her all the way down to her toes. Her heart began to race, and the awakening of some emotion she didn't quite understand coursed through her.

"Don't let me keep you," she said, keeping her features carefully composed. As if being alerted by his close scrutiny her heartbeat picked up speed.

"Oh, I won't, ma'am. I won't." He gave her a playful salute, and left.

Gloria resisted the temptation to slam the door behind him. Instead she closed it softly and leaned against it; she could hear him laughing, lingering on the other side. *Go away,* she commanded silently. When she put her ear to the door to listen more closely, he began singing in a hushed, low, surprisingly good imitation of Elvis Presley's voice: "Glo-ree-a, Glo-ree-a . . ."

"Gloria stood there for a long while after Jack walked away chuckling to himself. *What a strange, infuriating man,* she thought. *I could almost like him if . . . he didn't have that beard,* she admitted begrudgingly. Well, they wouldn't be seeing much of him, thank goodness, and Peter would soon forget him. They'd come West to start a new life and, damn it, she wasn't going to allow it to be complicated by an . . . aging hippie!

CHAPTER THREE

Gloria stayed in her room until she heard the sound of the motorcycle going down the highway. She was angry at herself for allowing Jack Evans to irritate her. What right did he have to voice her innermost feelings? Yes, she was scared. Dammit! She'd been scared, poor, and alone most of her life—that was one reason she'd grabbed at the carrot of security Marvin had dangled in front of her eyes. But she'd discovered there are things worse than not having financial security: being in a loveless relationship that was eroding her self-worth and crushing her spirit, for one. She was proud of herself for being able to break it off, then later finding the courage to leave Cincinnati and the rent-free apartment and the allowance paid into her account every month. She was on her own now, with a four-year-old son to support. If she was ever going to break free of Marvin's domination and stand on her own two feet, it was now.

She went out to the kitchen. The men had all left, and Ethel was cleaning up. Gloria carried the dishes from the table to the sink. Ethel rinsed them and stacked them in the dishwasher.

"That didn't take long," Ethel exclaimed when they

had finished. "Let's sit down, put our feet up, and have a good visit. I leave the vacancy sign on until about ten o'clock in the summer, then turn it off and go to bed."

Gloria followed her to the living room and watched as she knelt down to start a fire in the fireplace. "My, my. Here it is the first of September, and already the fire feels good in the evenings. We'll more than likely have snow flurries six weeks from now. It took me a while to get used to the winters here, but now I like the coziness of being snowed in, having a good fire going and a pot of chili on the stove." She tilted her head to one side and smiled at Gloria. "Do you think your old aunt has lost her mind?"

"Of course not." Gloria sat down on the couch and pulled her feet up under her caftan. "Fall is my favorite time of year. I love to watch the seasons change; I don't think I'd like to live where it's hot all year round."

Ethel sat down in the rocker and picked up a ball of yarn and a crochet hook, and pulled a half-finished afghan from the wooden bucket beside the chair. "There's somethin' about crochetin' that's relaxin'. I've made so many of these over the years, I can almost do it with my eyes closed."

"I'll always treasure the one you made for me, Aunt Ethel."

"Now that we've got some time to ourselves, tell me what finally pushed you into breaking away and coming out here. You said you wanted Peter to know that there was more to life than apartments and pavements and tall buildings. Is that all there was to it?"

"Yes, I wanted that, but I did it for myself too."

Gloria gazed into the fire, letting her memories wash over her. "When I look back on my life, Aunt Ethel, I find that the only constructive thing I've done has been to get Peter. Like I told you before, it was wanting a better life for him that gave me the courage to break away from Marvin in the first place." Gloria turned large, luminous amber eyes toward her aunt. "I knew immediately that I'd made a mistake marrying him. I didn't tell anyone. I just resigned myself to make the best of it."

"You stuck it out for five years. I'd give you an A for trying."

"I was a coward, and I still am to a certain degree. Marvin is powerful and ruthless. He provided me with all the material things as long as I was willing to be an invisible person in the house, a nonentity, and let his mother run things and not interfere in his life. I was merely one of the props of a production he created to show the world what a wonderful man he was. He went about his daily existence as if I wasn't there, until the occasion called for him to appear at some social function with a young, devoted wife on his arm. Then I was dressed up and put on display."

There was no bitterness in her voice, only a strange kind of sadness. She talked on as if compelled to tell it all.

"He was shocked and outraged when I announced I wanted to adopt an abandoned child. I found Peter while I was doing volunteer work at the center for abused children."

"I'm surprised he changed his mind."

"Marvin is a very strange man. To him appearance is everything. That was why he needed a wife and I guess he decided that adopting an abused child wouldn't hurt his image either." Gloria paused, and a picture of a man with thinning black hair, piercing blue eyes behind black-rimmed glasses, dark suit, white shirt, and conservative tie flashed across the screen of her mind. Suddenly there was another image superimposed over Marvin's—curly black hair, bushy beard, and laughing green eyes. Startled, Gloria shook her head to bring her thoughts back to what she was saying. "It's almost a requirement for a Masterson to do a certain amount of volunteer work among the less fortunate." The words were heavily laced with sarcasm.

Ethel clicked her tongue sympathetically.

"Marvin is the product of what he was raised to be. He was forty-five years old and had never been married when he married me. I was twenty-one. Aunt Ethel, I was so stupidly young and naive. Now I understand that was why he chose me. As the old saying goes—he swept me off my feet. If I had stopped to think for two minutes I would have realized we were from two different worlds and that I had mistaken security for love."

"Sometimes you have to flunk the course to learn the lesson," Ethel said dryly. "What did Ernest think about you marrying a man so much older than you?"

"He didn't meet him until the day of the wedding, and then we were off to Mexico City for our honeymoon. I don't think Daddy liked him much, but Mother was walking on clouds."

"Humph! That figures," Ethel said under her breath. Aloud she said, "Sometimes people are blinded by glitter."

"I wanted Peter so much," Gloria said. She bit her lower lip as she remembered. "He was so sweet and so helpless. I began to spend all day, every day, at the center. At first Marvin refused to even discuss the idea of adoption. He doesn't like children and has never wanted any of his own."

"What did he think when you left him?"

"By this time he was getting nervous that I might refuse to continue playacting as his wife. Besides, he was seeing a woman a few years older than himself. The fact that this woman had been married to someone on the fringe of European royalty was important to him. Marvin has a vast number of interests, the least of them being a physical relationship with a wife."

Ethel gave her a sideways glance, but Gloria had turned her face away. When next she looked at her aunt her eyes sparkled with devilish amusement.

"I heard that his new lady friend and Mother Masterson locked horns, and he had to end the relationship."

"Well, hallelujah!" Ethel chortled.

"I'm so glad I'm out of the whole mess. Aunt Ethel, I appreciate your letting me come here and giving me time to get on my feet and decide where to take my life from here on."

"This could be a new beginning for both of us. In a few years we could have a string of Rusty Cove motels all across the state."

Gloria giggled happily. "You'd better teach me how to clean the rooms first."

"We'll start on that in the morning, just as soon as the guests leave. The truckers are up and gone early,

52

the salesman a little later. I keep a pot of coffee, rolls, and cookies in the office, and they come in and help themselves before they go. Everyone who isn't staying over is usually out by ten o'clock. Gary rents number ten by the week and I make the bed when he's used it and change his bedding and clean the room on Friday, if it needs it."

"Do you wash everything here, or do you send it out?"

"We have a big washer and dryer in the room behind the kitchen. George got disgusted with the laundry service and went to town one day and ordered them. It took a hunk out of our savings, but now I'm glad we have them; they've already paid for themselves. Of course, when something goes wrong it costs an arm and a leg to have it fixed. But Gary's pretty good at fixin' things."

"Who stays here when you go to town? You must have a lot of grocery shopping to do."

"Gary is usually here on Saturday. He looks after things while I'm gone. He was here when George died; I don't know what I'd have done without him."

"Then he's the one you were telling me about on the phone? His wife died, and his little girl lives with his mother-in-law in Great Falls, right?"

"Yes. He lives in his truck when he's on the road. He dotes on that child, but knows she's better off with her grandma."

Gloria looked thoughtful.

"Aunt Ethel, do you know what I notice the most about this place? It's the quiet and the darkness. I stood on the porch for a few minutes before I came in, and there isn't a light anywhere except here at the motel. It's the strangest feeling to look out into all that black void."

"I guess I don't even notice it anymore. . . ." Ethel's head was resting against the back of the rocker, and her eyes were closed.

"Aunt Ethel, it's past ten o'clock. Do you want me to turn off the vacancy sign?"

Ethel didn't answer. Gloria got up from the couch just as her aunt opened her eyes, looked up at her, and shook her head as if to clear it.

"I must of dozed off." She put the half-finished afghan back in the bucket and got slowly to her feet, holding onto the chair.

"Are you all right?" Gloria asked anxiously. Her aunt didn't say anything. "Aunt Ethel, are you all right?"

"Just a little dizzy. Nothin' that hasn't happened a hundred times before. Too much excitement for an old lady, I guess." She straightened up. "See . . . it passed. I'm as good as new. You run along to bed and I'll turn off the vacancy light. Good heavens! It's later than I thought it was."

"I can turn off the lights, Aunt Ethel. What time do you get up?"

"Anywhere from 5:30 to 6:30, but you don't have to get up that early."

"I'll set my alarm for 5:30." Gloria put her arms around the small woman and hugged her. "Good night, Aunt Ethel. I . . . love you."

"Ah . . . go on with ya!" Ethel smiled embarrassedly. "Check the door and turn out the lights as you go through the office."

On her way out, Gloria looked back over her shoulder at her aunt, who was still standing beside the chair. A little, nagging fear possessed Gloria's heart. Had she imagined the white spots on each side of her aunt's mouth and the almost vacant look in her eyes when she first opened them? Had her words been slurred the slightest bit? She thought about it as she washed her face and pulled a nightgown over her head. Tomorrow, she decided firmly, I'm going to insist that she make an appointment with her doctor for a checkup.

Jack Evans sipped at the soft drink he had taken out of the refrigerator, and then wondered why he had taken it. He didn't want it; it was simply something to do. He considered building a fire in the potbellied stove in the center of the room, decided against it, and put on a jacket instead. He was restless tonight. It had been damned cold coming up that mountain road on the motorcycle; there'd been only a few times he'd let night catch him away from home unless he was in the jeep. The town seemed more forlorn than ever tonight. There had been no light in the saloon at the end of the dusty street when he came into town; old Cliff Rice, his sole neighbor, had either gone to bed, or had been too drunk to light the lamp.

Hangtown, Montana, population two: one old drunk and one worthless hippie, Jack mused. He sat down in a chair, tilted it back against the wall, and propped his feet on the table. Critical green eyes swept the neat but primitive home, surveying it as if through other eyes than his own. The bed on a headboardless frame, a three-burner stove for summer, a cookstove for winter, a table, a bookcase, a reading chair, and a gas-powered refrigerator-freezer made up the furnishings, along with a couple of standing TV trays. Every month he made a trip to Lewistown to get bottled gas to keep the lamp and refrigerator running.

Jack had a strong suspicion that the building he lived in had been a funeral parlor back in the 1870s. He had found a chest of moldy ribbons upstairs and a half-finished coffin in the shed out back. He had chosen the building because it had survived the ravages of time better than any of the other eleven buildings that made up the town, regardless of what it had been used for during the town's heyday.

Eight years ago he had founded the town, completely abandoned by all businesses and permanent residents, and bought it, not dreaming that, four years later, he would come back to the ghost town and call it home. Almost everyone thought he was a squatter, a hippie, or whatever they called bums these days. It didn't matter to him what anyone thought of him . . . that is, not until today. *Hell, it still doesn't matter,* he told himself, and the front legs of the chair he had tilted back against the wall came crashing down with a bang.

Dammit! What the hell is the matter with you, Evans? You acted like a love-sick kid today; you couldn't keep your eyes off the woman. The questions that had nagged at him all the way up the mountain continued to nag at him now. *Why in the hell did it irritate me when she looked at me as if I was something that had just crawled out of the sewer? I even enjoyed breaking that punk's arm when I found him harassing her and the kid, and God knows, I hate violence. And why did I have the urge to smash someone when the kid started to*

cry because I said I wasn't coming back to see him?
Dammit, Evans. Stay away from that woman and that
kid or you're letting yourself in for some sleepless
nights.

He placed his folded arms on the table and rested
his forehead on them. He sat that way for a long time
thinking, and trying not to think. Being with the boy
had brought forth a flood of memories that he had
managed to keep at bay for a long while. There had
been a time when he was sure he would lose his sanity;
now, he was more able to cope with his feelings. And
yet he was hearing, once again, the voice of his small,
green-eyed, golden-haired daughter: *I love you, Daddy.*
. . . I want to stay with you. . . . You'll come get me?
Promise me, Daddy—

"If only I'd've done things differently," he groaned
aloud. "If only I'd fought harder, dirtier, instead of
trying to be Mr. Nice Guy. Why in hell didn't I go
against the damn courts and just take her? I'd be in
prison now, but she'd be alive!"

The Chicago traffic was heavy the morning his attorney had called for him to come to his office. He had
filed a lawsuit against the FBI months ago, trying to
force them to tell him where they had secreted his
daughter, his ex-wife, and her new husband after the
man had testified and caused the conviction of the
head of a gigantic drug operation. He contended it was
a violation of his visitation rights that he was no
longer able to have Wendy with him every other week-
end.

He resisted every attempt of the FBI to force him to
drop the litigation. Naively he thought the courts

57

would give him custody of Wendy, at least for part of each year. But he had underestimated the power of the FBI. It had been almost a year since he filed the suit, and he had yet to have his day in court.

On the way to George's office he firmly believed the case was coming to trial, that George had good news. The moment he stepped into the office he knew that he was wrong. George Fisher, his attorney and friend, stood with his back to the door gazing out the window. A bald, overweight man with a cigar between his fingers pushed himself up out of one of the chairs and held out his hand.

"Mr. Evans, I'm Paul Blake of the FBI."

George turned from the window and came to stand before his desk. His face was gray and still.

"What's happened, George?" A feeling of dread began to overtake him; he felt the queer tension that hovered over the room. His first thought was: *Oh, my God! The judge has refused to hear the case.*

"Mr. Blake has something to tell you, Jack." There was anger in George's trembling voice.

The rotund man took a drag from his cigar, walked a few paces, and turned. "They found them. In spite of all we could do to ensure their safety, they found them."

"What do you mean?" Jack whispered hoarsely.

"I'm sorry, Evans. They planted a bomb in the car."

"Wendy?" Her name came out in a spasm of agony.

"All of them." The words were spoken quietly and with a finality that rocked his very soul.

A desolate silence followed while the enormity of the words sank into Jack's mind. Grief, then anger so black and great that it seemed to explode in his head, brought a roar of rage from his throat. He leapt to his feet and grabbed the fat man about the neck.

"You bastard! You goddammed bastard! You protected a goddamn criminal and let him kill my little girl! I'll kill you . . . I'll kill you—"

He came to much later on the floor. George was bending over him, holding a wet cloth to the large lump on the side of his head; he had been hit by the man's partner, who had burst into the room thinking that Jack was about to kill the man. Jack looked at George with dazed eyes, then rolled over, hid his face in his arms, and cried endless tears of despair.

A week later, after he had buried his daughter, he locked his house, mailed the key to George, and drove out of the city.

Even after four years there were still times when grief and frustration almost tore him apart. This was one of those times.

"Goddamn the law! Goddamn the courts, the FBI, and the whole stinkin', rotten system!" He lifted his head, shouted into the emptiness, and banged his fist down hard on the table, scattering papers and pencils.

Jack lowered his head miserably. His eyes flooded with tears as the memories came rushing back: silky blond hair in braids, sad green eyes, small arms about his neck, wet, sticky kisses on his face. After a while he turned out the light and felt his way in the dark to the bed, threw himself down on it, and prayed for the sleep that he knew wouldn't come.

He lay staring into the black night, the room silent except for the groaning of the floorboards when he shifted his weight on the bed. Out of the blackness came a woman's face, a perfect oval with a small fine nose and full soft lips, honey-gold hair, clear, tawny-gold eyes filled with fear and uncertainty. He felt a deep hunger for the companionship and sweetness of a woman to share his life. The lonely years stretched ahead—

"Get out of my mind," he whispered, almost savagely. "I don't *need* anyone and I don't *want* anyone."

By nine A.M. the motel and campgrounds were empty except for Gloria, Peter, and Ethel. Gary left on a run that would take at least five days. Before he left he promised that on his return he would fix Gloria's car, and he attached the U-Haul to the pickup so she could take it to Lewistown and turn it in.

Gary was a cheerful, easygoing man in his mid-thirties. There was almost a mother-son affection between himself and Ethel; he teased her, and she scolded him. He appeared to be genuinely glad Gloria and Peter had come to live with Ethel.

"The old girl needs someone with her," he confided to Gloria just before he climbed up into the cab of his big eighteen-wheeler. He handed her a card with the address and phone number of a freight center in Kansas City. "I'll be there most of the time. If you should need me, and I'm on the road, send word out on the CB; the truckers will pass it along."

Gloria felt a tingle of apprehension and looked over her shoulder to be sure they were alone before she spoke. "Do you think Aunt Ethel is . . . unwell?"

"She's slowed down a lot the last few weeks." He glanced over at where Ethel and Peter were putting a rope on the clothesline for the puppy. "She put on a good show last night for your benefit, but she's not up to running this place alone. I've tried to get her to see a doctor, but the old girl's got a mind of her own."

"Thank you for telling me. It confirms my suspicions. Do you know if she's had a checkup lately?"

"Not that I know of. She used to take the pickup to town on Saturday. But lately she's been giving me a list to fill when I go to Great Falls to see my little girl. I don't think she trusts herself to drive the pickup anymore." He climbed up into the cab and grinned at her. "I'm glad you're here. See ya on Friday."

Gloria went to stand beside Ethel and Peter, and waved to Gary as he pulled the big rig out onto the highway. The two long, powerful blasts of the horn delighted Peter, scared the puppy, and jarred Gloria's eardrums. She slipped the card he had given her into the pocket of her jeans and turned to look at her aunt. She was still looking at the truck, and she continued watching it until it went over the hill and out of sight.

The morning passed quickly. By lunchtime the rooms had been cleaned and the soiled linen piled in the laundry room. Gloria had done the majority of the work, over the protest of her aunt.

"I'll learn faster by doing than by watching, Aunt Ethel. Sit down and tell me what to do."

It wasn't until the middle of the afternoon, while Peter was napping and they were sitting at the kitchen table planning the evening meal, that Gloria had the opportunity to bring up the subject that had been on her mind all morning.

"Is your doctor in Lewistown or Great Falls, Aunt Ethel? I brought along Peter's medical records, and I

61

should get a doctor lined up for him. He'll need booster shots soon."

"I don't doctor much. But there's one in Lewistown, and it's closer. Is there something wrong with Peter?"

"No. But in case there is, I want a doctor who is acquainted with his medical history."

"Pshaw! What good'll that do? One's as good as 'nother when you're sick. They mostly guess, anyway." Ethel avoided Gloria's eyes and shuffled through a notebook of handwritten recipes.

"Aunt Ethel." Gloria uttered her aunt's name in a way that compelled the older woman to look at her. "When did you last see a doctor?"

"About a year after me'n George came here," Ethel answered staunchly. "We both went. George made me go."

"You haven't been back since?"

"I haven't been sick. Doctors don't know everything, by a long shot! Sometimes I think all they're good for is to set broken bones and sew up holes. They said George was fit as a fiddle, and a few months later he was dead. What'll happen'll happen, and there ain't no sense in worryin' about it."

"Will you go with me when I go to take Peter's records? I want to be sure you're all right, Aunt Ethel. You're . . . very dear to me."

"We'll see. Anyway, we have to wait until Gary's here before we both can leave," Ethel said with a perky smile, and Gloria knew her aunt's 'we'll see' meant no, she wouldn't go.

Ethel continued to chatter. "Now, what do you think about having Swiss steak for dinner? I'm looking for Harry and Neil tonight; they're truckers who make a run up to Kalispell every week. Bill Woler is due too; he's an auto supply salesman out of Bozeman. They'll call me on the CB when they get within calling distance, which in these mountains is about twenty miles out. And, you can't tell, we may have a tourist or two stop for the night. The weather is still nice. Although after school starts the bottom falls out of the tourist season."

Gloria knew her aunt was talking because the subject of going to the doctor had made her nervous. She said nothing more, deciding to wait until Gary was back to help in persuading her aunt to have the checkup.

Several days went by, and the pickup with the U-Haul attached still sat in the parking area. Gloria and Peter adjusted to life at the motel far more easily than she had imagined they would. She had no desire to go to town, and kept putting off the trip to return the trailer. In a couple of days the work pattern was established. Gloria insisted on doing all the cleaning, and Ethel filled the big washing machine and folded the clean laundry. Together they planned the evening meal and cooked it, Gloria maneuvering her aunt into the "sit-down" portion of the work. The time always passed very quickly.

Gloria had set boundaries for Peter, and he played happily with the puppy or rode his Big Wheel up and down the walk in front of the motel. The first few evenings found her exhausted, but it was a tiredness she welcomed. At night they watched a few hours of television, and then went to bed as soon as the VA-CANCY light was turned off.

Most of the people who stopped for the night had been guests of the motel before. The occasional new tourists who came by were usually those caught between towns late in the evening. Most of them were delighted with the home-cooked evening meal; it saved them from having to rely on snacks from the machines. Of course, there were exceptions.

The first night Gloria had charge of the desk, an older couple in a new Cadillac drove in and wanted to inspect the room before they signed the register. She understood their concern and cheerfully led them to the room, waiting patiently while they lifted the covers to see the condition of the mattress. They rejected two of the towels because of some small rust spots, and wanted paper to cover the toilet seat although Gloria assured them it had been washed that morning with disinfectant. They haughtily refused the offer of the evening meal, and when they turned in their key the next morning they just as haughtily refused the offer of coffee and fresh rolls. Gloria was glad to see the last of them, and secretly hoped they would get a flat tire before they reached Great Falls.

"Don't let 'em bother you," Ethel said. "For every one like them there are dozens of really nice people."

Peter asked Gloria several times when Jack was coming back. Whenever he heard the sound of a motorcycle coming down the highway, which wasn't often, he ran out to watch it pass, then turned away with a disappointed look. Gloria had to admit to a quickening of her own pulse when she heard the sound, and was sure that what she felt was relief when the cycle kept going instead of turning in to the drive.

On the fourth day, the day before Gary was due

back, Gloria heard the roar of a motorcycle coming from the west. Somehow she knew it would be *him*. She was right. She glanced out the window of the room she was cleaning and saw him turn in to the drive and stop in front of the office.

"Jack! Jack!" Peter jumped off his Big Wheel and ran to him as fast as his stubby little legs could carry him. They talked for a moment, and then Jack took off his helmet and set it down on the boy's head. He picked him up and carefully placed him on the seat in front of him, then rode around the circular drive several times before stopping in front of the office again and lifting the boy off. Gloria thought he would drive away, but he turned off the machine and put down the kickstand.

"Mom! Mom! Jack's here," Peter screeched as he ran down the walk.

"Don't shout, Peter." Gloria wheeled the vacuum cleaner out the door, down the walk, and into the next room.

"C'mon, Mom. Come see Jack."

"I've got to finish this room first. You run along." She unlooped the cord and plugged it into the outlet.

"Hurry, Mom. Jack! Jack!" he yelled. "Come see Cisco. Aunt Ethel says he needs a pen. She says he might get with a skunk if he goes to the woods. Can you stay for lunch, Jack?"

Gloria watched her son grab Jack's hand and drag him toward the door. She turned on the vacuum cleaner and moved it across the carpet vigorously while her mind churned. Damn that man! He wasn't the type of man she wanted as a role model for her son. *It's the motorcycle that fascinates Peter,* she told herself. Well, she'd put a stop to that! *It's disgusting for a grown man to be so oblivious to conventions that he'd let himself look like something that escaped from the zoo. No job, no responsibilities. What contribution would he ever make to society? How does he live? He's probably collecting a pension on some imaginary injury, letting the taxpayers support him.* She swept every inch of the carpet, several times, before she turned off the sweeper and leaned on the handle.

"*Va . . . room! Va . . . room!*" Peter's version of a roaring motor accompanied the rattle of the plastic toy he loved.

Gloria's eyes were drawn to the window. Peter, with the blue helmet on his head, was riding his Big Wheel down the walk, his small legs pumping energetically, pretending to be riding the black Harley-Davidson parked in the drive. *Being here* has *opened a whole new world for him,* she thought as she watched him. Having a puppy, being able to play in the dirt and shout without being chastised, and exploring among the trees were experiences he had not had before.

"Glory hallelujah! I thought you'd never turn that thing off."

Gloria spun around. Jack stood in the doorway. She had forgotten how big he was and how much hair he had. Today he wore a black jacket and a red bandana around his head. He stood looking at her, absently cleaning his nails with a long, thin-bladed knife. He tilted his head at an angle, his green eyes, full of amusement, holding hers.

Gloria pressed her lips tightly together, noting with disgust a gold earring dangling from his right ear, shining brightly against his black hair.

CHAPTER FOUR

"Hello, Glory. Aren't you about ready to hightail it back to the city?"

"Good morning, Mr. Evans." Gloria spoke lightly without looking at him and pulled the plug from the outlet, looped the cord over the sweeper handle, and pushed it determinedly toward the door.

"Peter said this was your last room." He stood there, his big frame blocking the doorway.

"It is, but I have other things to do. Excuse me. Please—"

"You didn't answer my question."

"No, I didn't. It's none of your business." She hated the nervous quiver in her voice.

"You're right." He chuckled. "I'm only curious." His eyes toured her figure in the faded jeans and the T-shirt, proclaiming in bright-red letters, YOU'VE COME A LONG WAY, BABY, that accentuated her small, firm breasts.

Gloria felt the heat that flushed her cheeks. She hated it when she blushed. It was his fault, and she wanted to slap him. He didn't budge from the doorway, so she backed off and smoothed the spread over the pillows on the bed in a purely superfluous gesture.

She gave the room a sweeping, critical glance to make sure everything was in place and moved toward the doorway again in a businesslike way, determined to not let this bear of a man intimidate her.

"You may not have anything to do, Mr. Evans, but I do. Please move out of the doorway." The nervous quiver was gone from her voice. It made her proud of herself and gave her the courage to lift her brows along with her small, pointed chin and look squarely into deep-set green eyes.

Jack looked down into twin pools of flashing amber lights. He could see a tiny mole on the lower lid of her right eye and a small puckered scar above her lip. It was faint, but showed plainly on the makeup-free skin of her face. That, and the fact that she couldn't weigh much more than a hundred pounds, gave her a child-like, vulnerable look.

Glory, Glory—sweet, sweet child. *Good grief,* he thought. *Did I say it aloud?* No, thank God, he hadn't. The tension-charged atmosphere had silenced him. *The way I feel right this minute,* he thought, *scares the hell out of me.*

Gloria shifted in acute discomfort. I'm crazy, purely crazy. The thought popped into her head and she wanted to laugh. Why do I always want to laugh when I'm with this man? A gray hair glinted here and there in the shiny black hair that curled about his ears and drooped down over the red band on his forehead. His beard was as glossy black as the brush of lashes that framed his green eyes, but with a sprinkling of silver. She could smell the faint odor of some spicy soap.

Gloria pressed her lips together and retreated a step so she didn't have to tilt her head so far back to look at him. Faded jeans were molded to his taut buttocks and long thighs. Their snug fit declared his sex in no uncertain terms; he was masculinity epitomized. She was brought out of her trance by an amused chuckle and made aware that she had looked at him too long and too hard.

"Do you like what you see?"

"Not . . . especially," she said lightly, feeling irritation at the fluttery sensation dancing in her stomach.

The twist of her lips produced a dimple, and Jack's gaze was drawn to it. There was something about this small, golden-eyed little redneck that compelled him to needle her, and he didn't understand it at all. Her body was dainty, compact, and utterly feminine. He fought down the urge to hold it against him, nuzzle her ear with his nose, taste the sweetness of her full lips.

She had persistently dogged his thoughts for the last few days. He had tried to clear his mind with hard, physical work by downing several dead trees he had saved to use for firewood. But even as he worked, thoughts of her danced in his head. After coming to within inches of his leg with the chain saw and barely missing his foot with the ax, he'd decided to purge himself of thoughts of her and ride over to the motel. After all, he reasoned, he'd promised the kid he'd come back to see him.

Now, as he watched her, he instinctively sensed the fawnlike unease she felt in his presence. *You stupid jackass!* he chided himself. *Why did you spend an hour making an old cuff link into an earring and why did you stop a mile up the road to put it on?* He chuckled as much at his own foolishness as he did at the look she had given him when she saw it.

"Hummmm . . ." He stroked his beard thoughtfully. "I take it you're not impressed with my good looks. I'm very impressed with yours. I like what I see very much."

"That just thrills me to death," she shot back curtly. "Are you hiding something under all that brush? Wrinkles? Sagging jowls? Ah . . . I bet it's a receding chin." A tiny amused curl of her lips accompanied the words.

"I've been told I'm very handsome," he retorted quickly, with brazen arrogance. He watched in fascination as the amber eyes changed from frosty stones to sparkling sunshine that penetrated his very soul, grabbed him, and shook him. "You're . . . very pretty when you smile." The words came out slowly, and he hadn't meant to say them. There was warmth in her eyes, and he suddenly wanted that warmth, needed it.

"I know it," she replied with a small shake of her tilted chin. Her lashes fanned down, then lifted over mischievous, laughing eyes.

Gloria's mental machinery, intent on maintaining an icy chill toward this . . . nonconformist, switched to lightness and laughter, and there wasn't a thing she could do about it. Her sense of humor took over, and before she realized it, she was completely out of control.

Watching as the laughter burst from her lips, Jack laughed too—a deep, rumbling, uncontrollable sound that he hadn't heard for so long it almost startled him. *Christ! You're like nothing I've ever seen before.* Again

70

he wondered if he'd spoken aloud and made an effort to gather in the threads of his scattered thoughts. There was an electric aura about her that threw his mind completely out of sync. *I've got to be careful of you,* he warned himself. *You could take more of a man's heart than he's willing to give.*

"Mom! Jack! Mom! Jack!" Peter squealed and squeezed through the door, grabbing Jack's jacket. "Cisco got away. He's lost in the woods."

"Oh, Peter. Aunt Ethel said to keep him tied up."

"I was bringin' him to see . . . Jack," he said with a downward turn of his quivering lips.

"No sweat, hotshot," Jack said calmly, and took Peter's hand. "He won't go far. What he needs is a pen. I wouldn't want to be tied to that clothesline all day, would you?" He glanced at Gloria's troubled face. "C'mon. We'll see what he's up to."

Gloria watched Peter skip happily alongside the big man. A thoughtful frown covered her features. It occurred to her that prejudices didn't come naturally. They were taught. Peter didn't care that Jack looked tough as rawhide, or that he lacked the ambition to hold a steady job, or that, provoked enough, he would deliberately break a man's arm. *Children are like animals when it comes to love,* she thought sadly. *They don't care if a person is old or young, slim or fat, smart or stupid, or if he has long hair and a beard. It's the way in which that person treats* them *that sets the tone of the relationship.* A bit of guilt laid itself on Gloria's conscience, and she didn't like the feeling at all.

Jack stayed for lunch, and afterward he and Peter left the kitchen to finish building a pen for Cisco that they had started with a roll of chicken wire they'd found in the shed. When they returned, Gloria and Ethel had finished the cleanup and were having a second cup of coffee. Gloria reminded Peter that it was time for his nap.

"But . . . Mom! Jack's here."

Jack sat down in a chair, and Peter wiggled his way between his knees and leaned against them.

"He'll be leaving soon. You know what will happen if you don't have your afternoon nap. You'll be too tired and too sleepy to eat your supper."

"Are ya goin', Jack? Are ya?"

"I wasn't planning on it, hotshot." Jack looked into Gloria's flashing eyes and smiled innocently.

"See, Mom! See! He's not going." Peter climbed onto Jack's lap.

"Well, that's just . . . dandy. Perhaps Mr. Evans will *still* be here when you wake up." Gloria got to her feet and held out her hand. "C'mon. You'll have to be washed. I think you've got most of Montana on your face and hands."

"Washed too?" Peter said dejectedly.

"Run along, sport. Moms get these crazy ideas about naps and baths, and there's not much a guy can do but go along with 'em." Jack nudged Peter's chin with his fist and lifted him off his lap.

"Don't go, Jack. You'll stay till I wake up?" Peter asked hopefully.

"Sure. I might even stay for supper if it's okay with Ethel." His eyes met Gloria's. She was looking at him as if she'd like to run him through with a saber. *She's mad as a hornet,* he thought gleefully. *She thinks I'm a bad influence on her son.* Absurdly he wished he hadn't lost his earring when he and Peter were building the pen. He'd have to pick up a supply at the dime store the next time he was in town. On second thought it might improve his image if he hung a few gold chains around his neck too.

"You're welcome anytime, Jack," Ethel declared. "I'll just throw in another potato or two. Anyhow, I want you to get on the roof before you go and tear that old bird's nest out of the dryer vent." She tried to keep from breaking into a smile. Something was going on between these two; a person would have to be deaf, dumb, and blind to not see the sparks they struck off in each other.

"Let's go, Peter," Gloria said sharply.

When Gloria returned to the kitchen she had showered and changed into a pair of forest-green slacks and a soft striped shirt with a small white, round collar. She had put on makeup for the first time since she and Peter arrived, and was carrying a jacket and a purse.

Jack was talking on the CB radio to his neighbor back in Hangtown, and Ethel was still sitting at the table.

"Break for that base station in Hangtown. Break. Break. Hey, Boozer, are you on the channel?"

"Yeah, I'm here, Bigfoot. Whatta ya want?" The slurred voice came in very faintly.

"Wiggle the squelch, Boozer. You're not coming in very clear."

"Ten-four. How's that?"

"Better. I'll not be back for a while. Ethel's new helper invited me to supper here at the Rustic Cove and you know I can't resist an invitation from a pretty woman." His amused green eyes watched Gloria's mouth tighten and her nostrils flare angrily. "Will you check to see if my hound has plenty of water and feed him along about sundown?"

"Ten-four, Bigfoot."

"And, Boozer, keep an eye on the road. You know what to do if you see the . . . feds," he murmured, his eyes full of mischievous laughter.

"The . . . what?"

"Feds, Boozer. The feds. Over and out," he said quickly, and put the microphone back on the hook. "And please don't burn down my town," he said silently to the dead mike.

"Break for that Bigfoot." Another voice came in on the set and Jack picked up the microphone again.

"You got the Bigfoot."

Gloria lifted her eyes to the ceiling in a gesture of impatience. *For crying out loud—the games grown men play! Bigfoot? I can think of a handle more suitable for him than that,* she thought. *Hummmm . . . How about Bushman, Hairy Harry, Blackbeard, Billy Whiskers, Montana DingBat?* As her mind churned, the impulse to giggle almost overwhelmed her. She turned her back to him, keeping it stiffly straight, until she could control her rebellious, smiling mouth.

"Red Baron, back atcha." The voice came over the speaker. "Tell Ma Brown I'll be there for chow and I'm hungry as a starved coyote."

"Ten-four, Red Baron. I'll pass the word to Ma Brown and that Barbie doll. There's roast beef in the oven and pie on the table. Keep 'er between the ditches, the rubber side down, and roll 'er on home."

"Obliged, Bigfoot. I'm gone."

"Dwight's always starved. I'll swear, I don't think

74

that man eats a bite all day when he knows he'll be here for supper." Ethel bounced up from the table to peer into the oven. The truckers were her family, and her boys were coming home for supper. Dwight Anderson, known as Red Baron on the CB, had been stopping every week for several years. She loved every one of her boys and worried about them when the weather was bad. Something Jack had said flashed through her mind, and she turned to smile happily at Gloria.

"You've got a CB handle," she exclaimed brightly. "Barbie doll fits you too. I got to hand it to you, Jack. When they were passin' out brains, you were right up front."

"And when they were passing out humility, he was at the end of the line," Gloria said heatedly. She ignored her aunt's What's-got-into-you look and whipped her jacket about her shoulders. "I'm going to take the U-Haul to town while Peter is napping, Aunt Ethel. Sit down and rest while I'm gone. I'll be back in plenty of time to help with dinner." She spun around and walked determinedly out the door.

"Hey, Glory. Wait a minute." She heard the screen door bang shut as she was going down the walk toward the pickup. "I think I'll come along."

She whirled around to face Jack. "And I think you won't." She opened the door of the truck, tossed her purse inside, and climbed up onto the seat.

"Oh, yes, I will." Jack grabbed the door and stopped her from closing it. "This old truck flops out of gear once in a while if you don't shift it just right. I'm not anxious to come rescue you *again,* Glory, Glory."

Gloria forced herself to count to ten before speaking, knowing that by using her name like that he was hoping she would lose her composure.

"I suppose you intend to hold that over my head for the rest of my life," she said calmly, but with an unmistakable edge in her voice. "It won't work. I don't feel the least bit obligated to you. I thanked you for your help. I offered to pay you. It's over and done with. Good-bye."

"At least we agree on one thing. Move over." He got into the truck and crowded her out from under the wheel.

"Just a doggone minute!" Gloria sputtered. "I don't want you to go with me."

"That's obvious. You'd rather swallow a toad than be seen in town with me, wouldn't you?" His eyes were twinkling merrily. "Glory, Glory . . . I'm the one taking the chance going off alone with you. How do I know you won't drag me off into the woods and have your way with me? You might come at me with a knife or an ax. You could be a psychopathic killer, a female Jack the Ripper who's killed hundreds of men in Ohio! Who knows what evil lurks behind that innocent face and beautiful wildcat eyes—"

"Fun-ny! You should be a comedian. But I suppose even *that* would be too much work for you." His teasing had fanned her temper, and her voice rose with heated anger.

"Could be," he said agreeably, and shrugged. "Give me the keys and we'll talk about it on the way to town."

Gloria's mouth opened, then snapped shut. Damned if she'd give him the satisfaction of an argument. She slapped the keys into his hand and slid over to the passenger side.

Jack put the truck in motion and they moved out onto the highway. She looked with pretended interest out the window, knowing that he was studying her, wondering why this bothered her so much.

"Glo-ry, glo-ry, hallelujah. Glo-ry, glo-ry, hallelujah . . ." he sang softly.

She refused to rise to the bait and continued to gaze stoically out the window.

The highway cut through a thick stand of spruce and pine. The sky overhead was a clear blue with a few puffy white clouds rolling lazily along on a slight breeze, and the air was clean and fresh. The long, magnificent sweep of landscape was green, yellow, and bronze; the colors glistened in the afternoon sun, providing a startling contrast to the blue sky above. It was all so breathtakingly beautiful. Gloria realized she could easily fall in love with this country, and now understood why her aunt had not wanted to leave it.

A tired sigh escaped her lips. Being constantly on guard with this man was energy consuming.

She turned to see Jack darting glances at her. He had rolled down the window, and the wind was whipping his hair back from his face. She studied the big man driving her aunt's truck and wondered why in the world the elderly woman trusted this unconventional screwball. She swung around and forced from her mind the thought that he really might be a handsome man beneath all that . . . brush.

"Does Peter look like his father? He certainly doesn't resemble you."

"No."

"She's a woman of few words," he said, as if talking to someone else. "But that's not all bad. A woman with her mouth flapping all the time would soon get on a man's nerves." He shot her a devilish look that fueled her temper again.

"If you think I'm going to tell you my life history, forget it," she snapped.

"I know part of it."

"You've been pumping my aunt for information!"

He laughed. "What I know about you, I heard before you got here."

"Then . . . you knew who I was when you stopped at the rest area," she said accusingly.

"I had a pretty good idea."

"Then why didn't you say so? And why ask about Peter's father? You must know that he's my adopted son and that he was left in the rest room of a sleazy tavern—an abused, frightened child who was picked up by the police and brought to the center for abandoned children. He had never been loved or wanted, held or cuddled . . ." Her voice rose with an anger that had nothing to do with him. She looked into his eyes and was startled by the tenderness she saw there.

"I didn't know that," he said slowly.

They lapsed into silence. During this time they passed the rest area where he had beaten up the two hoodlums who had harassed her. She glanced at him. The flip manner was gone. His brows were drawn together as if in deep concentration. She looked away from him and allowed her eyes to feast on the panorama stretched out before her: forest-covered slopes that after a while gave way to the cluster of buildings that made up the town of Lewistown.

There was a soft quality to the afternoon light as it filtered through the windshield of the truck, evidence of the autumn sun's waning strength. To Gloria this peaceful scene seemed a million miles away from the crowded and sometimes smoggy streets of Cincinnati.

The pickup bounced over the railroad tracks and down the long main street of the town. Other streets branched off at intervals, dividing groups of stores, some of which were faced in brick. A new modern bank sprawled on a corner, reminding Gloria of Marvin. Banks always have the newest and the most modern-looking buildings in town, she mused.

A white church, its cupola stark against a background of trees whose leaves were faded green, muted rust, and brilliant gold, was set back on a side street looking stately and serene.

Jack turned the truck into the drive of a service station. Along one side was a row of rental trailers and trucks. He pulled into that area and stopped.

"Give me your papers."

It wasn't *Do you want me to take care of it for you?* It was simply *Give me your papers.* She fought down the resentment that bubbled up and gave him a searing glance. With her chin set at a stubborn angle she opened the door, got out, and went into the office. She had rented the trailer and she would turn it in without any help from "Bushman," she thought with an impulse to giggle in spite of her irritation.

When Gloria returned to the pickup, the trailer had been unhitched and moved away. Jack was not in sight, and her first impulse was to slide beneath the wheel and drive away. But when she reached to start the motor, she realized that the keys were not in the ignition. Damn! He was taking no chances on being left in town.

Frustrated, knowing that he had anticipated what she would do if she had the chance, she sat in the truck and watched the cars come in, fill with gas, and leave. Five minutes went by and then ten. She fidgeted on the seat, looked at her watch, and tapped her foot against the floorboard of the truck. *Damn him!* I should have expected this, she mumbled to herself. Isn't this typical of a loafer, a good-for-nothing? *He* has all the time in the world, she fumed. Time means nothing to *him*. *He* isn't doing anything.

Her temper was on the verge of skyrocketing when she saw him saunter out of the service station where the mechanics were working on cars and walk in lei-surely fashion toward the truck. He opened the door, hopped in, and grinned at her. At least she thought it was a grin, judging by the creases at the corners of his eyes.

"Did you get things squared away?" The amuse-ment in his eyes was undeniable, and his smug attitude made her all the more determined not to allow him to goad her to anger.

"Of course," she answered with a haughty lift of her brows.

"Hungry?"

"No. We just ate lunch."

"That was a couple of hours ago, Glory. Let's grab a hamburger and a beer."

"No. I want to go home."

His green eyes roamed over her face, taking in the shining nose, windblown hair, and tight-lipped mouth.

He reached out and covered with one of his the hands she had clasped in her lap.

"Don't worry. You look just fine," he said in a reassuring tone. "I'd not be ashamed to take you into any restaurant in town."

"Well . . . that's big of you," she sputtered, and yanked her hand from beneath his. "You're going to drive me out of my mind! Do you know that? I'm not hungry. I want to go home. Spelled h-o-m-e. Can't you get that through your thick head?"

"Ah, ah, ah . . . temper, temper," he chided gently, as if she were a child. "You need to eat, Glory. You're as skinny as a starved alley cat and as cross as a junkyard dog." He boldly stared at the length of her figure and he shook his head sadly.

"Oh, my God!"

"It's not ladylike to swear, darlin'." He started the motor and they moved out onto the street. "We'll go to a hangout of mine. It's down by the tracks. It's usually pretty tame during the day, but at night— *wow!* It's every fantasy a guy dreams about. They serve everything from a little Coke, ah . . . er . . . Coca Cola, to rustled steak not a day off the range. And the girls upstairs . . . Ooops, sorry, you'd not be interested in them." He glanced at her, but all he could see was the back of her head. She was staring out the side window. "If you're worryin' about how you look, Glory—don't." His voice rambled on with exaggerated patience. "The people down there are pretty tolerant of 'straights.' But you could unbutton that shirt a little and show a little bosom. That way you'd not be quite so conspicuous."

This man was crazy! No longer able to control her

anger she spun around to face him. The smug look on his face caused her to clench her fist and do something she'd not dreamed she was capable of doing. She hit him a resounding blow on the upper arm.

"If I were a man, I'd beat you up!" Her poise completely abandoned her, and she heard herself shouting. It felt so good to yell, she did it again. "Ohhhh . . . you smart-ass! You make me so mad. You're the most aggravating creature I've ever met. You're a nineteen sixties hippie living in the eighties. You're impossible, rude, and . . . a lazy, no-good deadbeat." She stopped, then took a deep breath. Her pulses were thudding like a jackhammer in her head. This oversized teddy bear was driving her out of her mind and she desperately needed to be delivered from his presence.

"Atta girl. Let it all out. It feels good to yell, doesn't it? I do it sometimes when I feel uptight," he murmured, his eyes bouncing from her to the street and back again. "I walk out into the middle of Hangtown, face the empty buildings that once made up a town of over a thousand hardy souls, and I yell as loud and as long as I want to. It's good for the heart, the lungs, and the digestive system. If a person lets off steam once in a while it'll keep 'im from getting an ulcer. It also helps if you've got something to kick," he added with green eyes dancing and his mouth curving into a grin.

Gloria stared back at him and desperately tried to hold on to her anger. Unwelcome thoughts trampled through her mind. She had never seen such eyes on a man. Between the spread of black lashes they were as green as a new leaf in the spring. There was strength and stubbornness there, just as there was in his hard, muscled body. Yet they were so soft and so deep, seeming to contain a knowledge about her that was strangely disconcerting. It was as if he knew everything about her—everything, from her childhood to her sheltered life as Marvin's wife. He even knew that she was repelled by, yet attracted to him. She swallowed, feeling a sudden aching tightness in her throat.

"Jack Evans," she said quietly. "You're . . . giving me a headache."

CHAPTER FIVE

Jack turned onto a street that ran parallel with the railroad tracks.

"What's the matter with you? You didn't pay one bit of attention to me when I said I wanted to go home," Gloria said, her voice hard with irritation.

"Yes, I did. I heard you loud and clear." They bounced onto a graveled drive and he parked the truck beside a frame building with beer signs nailed to the siding on each side of the door and a weathered swinging sign above. "You said you weren't hungry. You said you wanted to go home. You said I was giving you a headache. See there? I'm no dummy."

"That's your opinion."

"I'm starved," he said, ignoring her sarcasm. "That bacon-and-tomato sandwich you gave me for lunch didn't amount to anything. It'll only take a few minutes to have a hamburger and a beer." He made it sound quite sensible.

"I'll wait out here."

"Stubborn little mule," he murmured, and the intensity of his gaze caused her to blush, but she returned his look steadily. He opened his shirt pocket and dropped the truck keys inside. "Suit yourself. But it'll take much longer for me to eat if you're not with me."

"Are you blackmailing me?"

"Uh-huh."

Gloria jerked at the door handle. "That figures. C'mon, let's get it over with."

"Wow! Such enthusiasm." Jack met her at the front of the truck and attempted to take her arm, but she jerked it away. He was chuckling as they entered the café.

Gloria headed straight for the first booth and dropped down on the red vinyl padded seat. Jack eased his bulk into the seat opposite her. His knees touched hers and she moved over next to the wall and placed her purse on the seat beside her. She looked around the room to keep from looking at him.

Three men—ranchers, by the look of the wide-brimmed hats pushed to the back of their heads and the boot heels hooked over the braces of the stools—sat at the counter. The other five booths and the four tables between the booths and the counter were empty, but all were laid with heavy white china, the cups turned upside down on the saucers and the silver for each place setting folded neatly in a paper napkin. The men at the bar glanced at them and then continued eating. The woman behind the counter drew two glasses of water and, carrying both in one hand and a menu under her arm, came to the booth.

"Hi, Jack. How're ya doin'?"

"Fine, Helen. You?"

"Fine."

The woman looked down at Gloria and smiled. She was tall, blond, and large boned, with every hair stiffly in place. She was past middle age, but her lined face was carefully made up, her white uniform and low-wedge shoes spotlessly clean.

Gloria noticed her hands as she placed the menu on the table in front of her. They were large, capable, work-worn hands that told her life hadn't been easy for this woman. She returned her friendly smile, accepted the menu, and murmured, "Thank you."

"This is Gloria, Helen. She came to give Ethel a hand at the motel . . . for a while." Jack added the last words with a measured, narrow-eyed glance at Gloria before he opened the menu.

"That's nice. I'm glad Ethel will have some help. She looked peaked and tired the last time she was here." Helen spoke with such sincere concern that Gloria looked up in surprise.

"Do you know my aunt?"

"Know Ethel? Mercy! I've known that woman since the day she and George bought that motel. My land! So you're the niece from Cincinnati she's talked about so much. Welcome to Montana. I hope you like cold weather; it can be a bear here at times."

"I'm used to cold weather. It won't bother me at all."

"We'll see about that," Jack murmured with his eyes on the menu. Gloria pursed her lips stubbornly.

"What'll you have, Jack?" Helen's gaze bounced between Gloria and Jack, and her brows drew together in a puzzled frown. She added, "You know what we've got without looking at the menu. Heavens! You've been eating here for several years."

"Give us a couple of hamburgers and a piece of pie. Glory needs to be fattened up if she's going to stand up to the work out at the motel." He looked into Gloria's resentful amber eyes steadily. "Make mine apple. What kind do you want? Helen makes the best pie in the state."

"I told you I didn't want anything. I'm not hungry." She gave Jack a searing glance before she looked up at Helen. "I'll have a cup of coffee, please."

"Two hamburgers, two pieces of apple pie, and a pot of coffee." Jack handed the menu back to Helen. "Glory's being contrary again. She hardly ate anything for lunch. I think she's one of those women who're afraid they'll get drumstick thighs," he added in a loud whisper and with a conspiratorial wink.

Helen hesitated. "Now, Jack, quit your funning. If she—"

"If she doesn't eat it, I will," he said pleasantly.

"Suit yourself." Helen lifted her shoulders and walked away. Jack's eyes wandered around the room before coming back to Gloria's frozen features.

"Do you practice being rude, or does it just come naturally to you?" Gloria was so angry her voice trembled, but she made herself look him directly in the eyes. "I don't have a weight problem. I've *never* had a weight problem. And if I did, anyone with any manners at all wouldn't comment on it."

"That got to you, didn't it?" He raised his eyebrows.

"And . . . you led me to believe this was a . . . hangout for thugs and . . . and . . . drug users!" She felt the color rise in her cheeks as she spoke, so she looked out the window, afraid that if she continued to look at him, the gleam in his eyes would goad her to hit him again.

"I told you what you expected to hear," he said, and there was laughter in his voice. "You've come from a nice, orderly, sheltered little world where you were taught to be wary and look down your pretty little nose at an uncouth character like me. Just because I don't fit into the mold of what you think is 'respectable,' you shoved me into the 'undesirable' category." He chuckled. "Glory, Glory, this is the nineteen eighties. People are more tolerant now of us . . . hippies."

She turned to look at him. Her anger was replaced with quiet dignity. "Don't laugh at me and don't analyze my life. You know nothing about it! You may think me naive for a woman my age, and that may be true to a certain extent. But I have my principles just the same. I'm just learning to stand on my own two feet after five years of being told, do this, do that—eat this, eat that—wear this, wear that. I was brainwashed into thinking I had to be subservient to a man's wishes. That's over—done with—finished! I'm a person in my own right, with my own opinions, and I'm perfectly capable of making my own decisions without help from you or . . . anyone." At the end she was striving to keep her tone level and her lips from trembling, but her traitorous voice betrayed her on the last word. She felt the tears rising and looked away from him.

"I'm sorry. It wasn't my intention to make fun of you." The softness of his voice was like a caress, and brought her eyes back to him. A faint frown pleated his brow, and his eyes, full of concern, were fastened on her face. She stared into their depths, and her mind went blank. She found herself tongue tied and couldn't remember the rest of what she had wanted to say.

She looked away from him to some distant spot behind his head and willed her eyes to stay dry. Heartache parted her lips and she gulped small gasps of air into her lungs. She wished desperately that she were back at the motel. This bearded man disturbed her in more ways than she cared to acknowledge. He could make her reveal more about herself than she wanted him to know. She'd never met anyone quite so vibrant, so aggressively masculine, in her life. At times he was like a gentle giant. He attracted her, confused her, angered her, and made her feel achingly alive and feminine, something no other man had ever done. His smile and warm, caressing voice caused an unwelcome glow of happiness to start in her knees and work its way up to her chest.

They sat silently while Jack mentally kicked himself for having caused the pain reflected in her wide amber eyes. More than anything he wanted to cradle her face in his hands, bring her head to his shoulder, and comfort her. For a few moments he was completely honest with himself. She was a lovely woman, very desirable. He wanted to hold her and to kiss her. He wanted her to look at him with bright laughter in her eyes instead of the pain he saw there now. For the first time in years he wanted more from a woman than the quick satisfaction of a primitive desire. He wanted her mind, her body, her . . . love. The knowledge hit him with the force of a hurricane. *Christ! You stupid bastard! The last thing you need is a woman to complicate your life.*

Helen brought their food, and without conscious thought of what she was doing, Gloria picked up the hamburger and began to eat. It was half consumed before she realized how hungry she was. She glanced at Jack, fully expecting to find him watching her with a taunting gleam in his eyes, but he was concentrating on his food. She glanced at the hands that held the sandwich. His fingers were long and slim and tipped with blunt, clean nails. A thin gold watch was nestled in the fine black hair on his wrist.

Jack looked up and met her gaze. "What are you thinking while those amber eyes are boring holes through me?" His voice was soft, without the slightest hint of sarcasm.

"What are *you* thinking?" she replied, unwilling to answer his question.

"I'm thinking you have the most beautiful eyes I've ever seen." His voice was lower than before and his eyes had darkened to a clear jade.

"Thank you." She was flustered at this unexpected turn in the conversation, but absurdly pleased by his compliment.

They didn't speak again until they had finished their meal, then Jack said, "Ready?"

Gloria nodded. He went to the register and waited for Helen to finish pouring coffee for the cowboys. One of them spoke to him.

"How're ya doin', Jack?"

"Pretty good, Roy. You got them mangy old steer of yours ready for shipping?"

"Just about."

The man cast admiring glances at Gloria, who was now standing beside the door. His look invited an introduction; Jack ignored it and turned his attention to digging bills out of his jeans pocket. The cowboy had a dark, weathered face, light-brown hair, and a long, slim body. His eyes were frankly admiring as they toured Gloria's trim figure. When she met his gaze, he smiled, and his face lit up with charm. He nodded to her and narrowed his eyes in a way that said he would like to know her, but she turned away.

Gloria climbed into the dusty pickup and wondered idly if comfortable cars were banned in this part of the country. Almost everyone drove either a pickup truck or some other type of four-wheel-drive equipment. After five years of riding in Lincolns and Cadillacs, it had taken her a while to get used to her small compact car, which was a luxury compared to this jolting truck.

They were headed down the highway toward the motel before Jack spoke.

"Roy considers himself God's gift to the ladies. You'd be smart to not encourage him." He spoke softly, but his words were accompanied by a cool look.

"Is he married?"

"No. But he's on his fourth or fifth 'live-in,' as far as I know."

"Does he own a big ranch?" Sensing his irritation, some little devil in Gloria prodded her to ask the question.

Jack's head swiveled around and he eyed her unsmilingly. "His pa owns the ranch. Roy'll have to share it with a raft of brothers and sisters. That is, if there's anything left to inherit."

"Does he live on the ranch?"

"In a trailer house. He needs his privacy." There wasn't a trace of humor in his voice.

"Does his family approve of his 'live-ins'?"

"I don't know, I haven't asked them. Why all the questions? Are you thinking of making a play for Roy?"

The bitterness in his voice caused her to look at him sharply. His brows were drawn together in a deep frown of disapproval; suddenly the fun had gone out of the game. Without answering his question she turned to stare out the window.

There were a million questions floating around in her mind. Who was Jack Evans? What had happened to cause him to drop out of the mainstream and live this unconventional life-style? Why was he so hostile all of a sudden? Why wasn't she feeling elated because she had, at last, managed to get under his thick skin and irritate him? Was he angry because the cowboy had flirted with her? Did he think she was so shallow that she'd be flattered by the man's rakish attention?

The highway from the rest area to the motel seemed infinitely shorter than it had the day she'd ridden over it with Jack on the motorcycle. Still, it was full of hills and curves, and Gloria was relieved when she could see the familiar orange doors of the motel.

The truck rattled over the metal bridge that covered the drainage ditch and proceeded through the empty parking area. Dusk had settled, and Gloria vaguely wondered why Aunt Ethel hadn't turned on the office lights. Jack braked to a stop just short of the yawning doors of the shed where Ethel parked the truck. Gloria got out without a word or a backward glance. The back door of the motel slammed shut, and Peter ran to meet her.

"Mom! Mom! I c-couldn't f-find you!" Ragged, desperate sobs accompanied his frantic words. Tears streaked his face. He grabbed her around the legs and held on.

"Oh, honey! Didn't Aunt Ethel tell you I went to Lewistown to take the U-Haul back?" She dropped her purse, knelt down beside him, and hugged him to her. "There, there, don't cry. I should have told you I was going."

"I was s-scared," he stammered.

"There was nothing to be scared about. You knew I'd be back. Aunt Ethel was with you."

"Aunt Ethel is sleepin'. I made noise, but she didn't wake up. People called on the radio and she didn't wake up."

"Aunt Ethel is . . . sleeping? At five o'clock?"

Gloria blanched, remembering that her aunt never napped, and a cold hand of fear began to squeeze the breath out of her.

"Oh, my God!" She loosened herself from Peter's clinging arms and ran to the door. "Aunt Ethel! Aunt Ethel!"

The kitchen was dark and she fumbled with the light switch. She went quickly through the swinging doors to the living area, switched on another light, then stopped short, the back of her hand going to her mouth.

Her aunt lay on the couch with an arm hanging down, palm out. Her mouth was open and twisted to the side. Gloria leaned over her. She was so pale and still. Fear shattered her heart. No! No! Oh, dear God! Don't let her be . . . dead! Her mind raced, imagining the worst.

"Jack!" Her scream was like a lost wail. In blind

93

panic she ran to the back door. "Jack!" She sucked air into her lungs in jerky gasps. "Come quick! Aunt Ethel—"

Jack shot past her with Peter clinging to his neck. When he reached the couch he set Peter on his feet, and the distraught child flung himself against his mother's legs, sobbing helplessly. Gloria fell on her knees and gathered him to her.

"Hush, darling, hush. Please hush," she begged.

Jack searched Ethel's wrist for a pulse and lifted her eyelid. Then he got to his feet.

"She's alive," Jack murmured gently, and a feeling of relief and gratitude flooded Gloria's numbed senses. "I think she's had a stroke."

"We've got to get her to the hospital. I'll call an ambulance."

"It'll take an hour for an ambulance to get here and back." Jack put a reassuring hand on Gloria's shoulder. "Gary's car is in the shed. I'll get the master key from the office and unlock his room—the car keys are bound to be there. Lock up the front and leave a note on the table for him; he and Dwight should be here soon. Then gather up a bunch of blankets and a couple of pillows." He was gone before Gloria could get to her feet.

"Aunt Ethel is sick, Peter. You're going to have to help us get her to the hospital. Go put on your jacket and bring the pillow from my bed." The child stood there sniffling. "You're a big boy, and . . . Jack and I need you. Hurry now." Her words seemed to calm him, and he ran toward their room.

Gloria scribbled a brief note to Gary, put it on the kitchen table, and went to her aunt's bedroom. She took several blankets from the closet shelf. She thanked God Jack was with her; her mind was so fettered with fear that she was only half aware of what she was doing. Peter returned, and with trembling hands she helped him into his jacket.

"Take the pillow to the back door and wait for Jack, honey. Oh, I'm so glad I have you to help me."

"I love Aunt Ethel."

"I love her, too, honey," Gloria said, zipping up his jacket and hugging him briefly.

"Will she get a shot?" he asked gravely.

"I don't know, love. We'll have to wait and see."

Jack parked the big sedan just a few steps from the back door. Gloria spread pillows on the backseat, and Jack carried Ethel out to the car. He gently laid her down on the seat and covered her with blankets. Gloria climbed in and sat beside her aunt. Jack lifted Peter into the front and fastened the seat belt around him.

"You sit up here with me, hotshot, and hold Aunt Ethel's pocketbook. There may be things in there the hospital will want to know." He put the car in gear and drove out onto the highway.

Less than five miles down the road they met Gary headed for the motel. Jack pressed on the horn, blinked the car lights, and sped on past. Gloria glanced out the rear window to see the brake lights come on the big eighteen-wheeler, then go off as Gary speeded up again. She wondered what he thought at seeing his own car go racing toward town.

Gloria teetered on the edge of the seat, holding her aunt's hand. She had no idea of how she would have reacted to this emergency if she had been there alone. She wanted to talk, wanted to tell Jack how grateful she was that he was with her, but she remained silent, and the big car ate up the miles.

They reached the railroad tracks at the edge of town and Jack slowed the car to ease over them, then turned onto a wide, tree-lined side street; at the end of it was a large gray building. At one side was a circular drive that passed under an enclosure with a large bold sign that said EMERGENCY ONLY. Jack drove the car in, stopped, and pressed on the horn before he got out. A white-coated orderly met him at the door and, after a few words from Jack, turned back to call for a stretcher.

Although she felt nervous and sick, Gloria managed to walk calmly down the corridor to the admittance desk and answer the questions they asked about her aunt. She was terribly glad Jack had thought to bring Aunt Ethel's purse; from it she extracted her insurance card, social security card, and driver's license. She fidgeted while the woman took what seemed like an eternity to note down the information. Her fear grew with each passing second. When the woman was finally done she hurried back to the room where Jack and Peter waited—wanting, *needing,* the security of Jack's calm presence.

She stood in the doorway and watched Jack cuddle Peter in his arms. The child was asleep, and Jack was shifting him so his head lay comfortably in the crook of his arm.

"He didn't have any dinner," Gloria said absently.

"I got him a sandwich from the vending machine, but he was asleep before he could eat the whole thing. Did you get Ethel checked in?"

"Yes. Has the doctor said anything?"

"He said they had put her on life support systems, and that another doctor had been called in. Sit down, Gloria. We can't do anything but wait."

She sat down with a deep sigh, and when he reached for her hand she curled her fingers tightly around his and gripped hard. The warmth and closeness were comforting. She suddenly longed to cuddle against him, as Peter was doing, and absorb his strength.

Time flew past as they sat on the couch, hands clasped, Gloria's shoulder against his.

"Jack," she whispered softly, unaware of the intimacy of her tone. "I don't know what I'll do if anything happens to Aunt Ethel. She means a lot to me."

"You'll just have to do the best you can, Glory. We all have an inner strength we don't even know we possess; that's how we endure times of terrible grief."

"I'm glad you're with me." She looked up at him, her eyes flooding with tears.

"I'm glad I am too. Are you hungry? I ate what was left of Peter's sandwich, but I can get another one from the dispenser. And there's coffee too."

"I don't know if I could eat or not, but I could use the coffee. But don't you think you should call Gary?"

"I thought I'd wait until I had something definite to tell him. I'll lay Peter on the other couch and get some coffee."

After Jack had left the waiting room, Gloria reached for a magazine and began flipping through the pages, hardly reading a word. She was filled with apprehension, her heart fluttering and her fingers trembling as she turned the pages, her ears attuned to the sound of footsteps. The waiting seemed to be more agonizing without Jack; it was easier when he was there to share it with her. She threw the magazine down onto the table and went to the door. At the end of the long hall a white-coated orderly was pushing a cart. She was surprised at the lack of activity, then remembered the time of day and the fact that this was a small hospital, unlike the busy hospitals in Cincinnati where she had occasionally taken children from the center where she worked.

She was very glad when Jack's big frame filled the doorway. His eyes searched her eyes, asking the question: "Any news?"

She shook her head despairingly. "No one has come at all."

He looked down at her tired, pale face, her dark-circled eyes dulled with fatigue. He had never longed to hold, or kiss, or comfort a woman so badly. She was so small, and looked so forlorn sitting there. He desperately wanted to see her eyes bright with laughter, her chin tilted proudly, her cheeks dimpling merrily.

Jack felt suspended as he stood looking down at her. He was unable to understand or accept the overpowering protective feeling that swept over him. A corner of his heart that had never been filled was suddenly overflowing. Almost in a daze he held out the foam cup.

Gloria accepted the coffee with a bleak smile of thanks.

"It seems like we've been waiting forever," she said in a choked, tired voice.

"It hasn't been an hour, Glory. We'll know something soon."

They sat close together on the couch, and when Jack felt a shiver run through her slight body, he took off his jacket and draped it about her shoulders.

His arm stayed about her to hug her to his side.

CHAPTER SIX

It was past midnight. Jack wrapped his jacket around the sleeping child and carried him out to the car. Gloria walked beside him. The air was crisp and cool, the moon clear and bright. He placed the child on the backseat and covered him with the blankets. And then he turned to Gloria and put his jacket about her shoulders.

"No. You'll need it."

"Get in. I'll get the heater going."

He opened the door and she slid under the wheel to the other side. She watched him in the flashing lights of a passing car; his face was turned toward her as he inserted the key to start the motor. It was incredible that in just a few hours' time her feelings for him had changed so drastically.

"Move over close to me and we'll keep each other warm until the heater gets going." His voice came softly out of the darkness over the purr of the engine.

"You can have your jacket." She was suddenly flustered and at a loss for words. Her gaze was drawn to the shadowed outline of his face and his eyes gleaming at her through the darkness.

"C'mon. Move over." His hand was on her knee.

"Closer," he commanded softly after she had moved a few inches toward him. "You're shivering." She moved again, and he adjusted his own position until her shoulder was tucked behind his and her hip, leg, and thigh fit snugly along his muscular length. "That's better. You'll be warm soon." He shifted the gears and put the car into motion. "We'll be home before you know it, and I'll make us a cup of hot chocolate."

After they had driven a few blocks, the lights of the town were left behind. Gloria looked straight ahead at the road; she thought about her aunt's condition and willed herself to not panic. Jack placed his hand in her lap; without hesitation she pressed her palm against his, and his fingers entwined with hers.

"I like holding your hand, Glory."

"Thank you for being with me tonight." It was pleasant, comforting, to be with him. She was weary in mind and weary in body, and hovered against his masculine strength in a dreamlike state. She felt . . . sheltered, cherished. His hand was like a lifeline in a storm.

He briefly released her hand to adjust the heater, then blindly sought it again. She clasped it and laced her fingers through his.

"You do realize that Ethel may never be completely well again even if she does come through this crisis?"

"Yes, I know that," she answered in a small voice. "Oh, Jack, she'll never speak again."

"The doctor said there was the *possibility* of that. It's not a certainty. She had a massive stroke, and they'll not be sure of the damage for several days. She knew that you were there and that she wasn't alone. I'm sure that meant a lot to her."

"I'll try to keep the motel going until she can decide what she wants to do with it," she whispered huskily.

Jack was quiet. The car sped along the highway with only the sound of the motor filling the moonlit silence of the night. He needed time to sort out his emotions, untangle his confused thoughts, and decide what he *really* wanted out of life. The feelings he had for this woman scared the hell out of him. It was a shock to him to realize that he'd never felt so complete as he had sitting beside her at the hospital, his arm holding her close, sharing her anxiety as they waited for the doctor. All he'd wanted to do, then, was to be with her, comfort her, take care of her. *Now* he wanted to kiss her with her arms about his neck. He wanted to hold her hips in his hands and feel her breasts against his naked chest, have her to *want* him. *Dammit, Evans, don't think about it! She doesn't feel that way about you.*

"You can't run the motel by yourself," he said, struggling to get his mind back to reality.

"I'll have to."

"I'm not sure it's a good idea for you and Peter to be out there alone. Gary's gone five nights a week, and there's all kinds of riffraff traveling the highway."

"I know. I've met some of them. Remember?" She glanced at him and saw the frown creasing his brow. "But if Aunt Ethel could handle them, I can."

"Ethel is not young and beautiful."

"Should I thank you for a compliment?"

He searched her features for a trace of sarcasm and found none. Rather, she was trying to suppress a grin. He glanced at the road ahead, then back to her soft

102

mouth and glowing eyes. A lovely, leaping flame of desire flickered through him.

"No," he said slowly while his mind ached to say something else. "I wouldn't want you to slip out of character."

That brought an unexpected trill of laughter. "Have I been that bad?"

"You've been a regular shrew," he murmured teasingly.

"Well, what about you? You irritated me something awful!" Her smile jarred his senses.

"I did bug you a bit, didn't I?" He chuckled softly.

"Yes, you did."

He glanced down at her. Her image stayed with him when he turned back to watch the road. She looked so damned fragile. Her face was pale in the moonlight, her lips quivering, her eyes dancing with more enjoyment than he'd ever seen, yet still full of vulnerability. When she laughed, the musical sound struck a chord deep in a part of him that he had thought was closed off forever.

"Jack . . ." Her voice was low, her face close to his shoulder. He knew she was looking at his profile. "I really do appreciate having you with me tonight. And . . . I'm sorry for the nasty things I said about . . . your appearance and your life-style. I guess I'm what you'd consider . . . super-straight."

"It's all right, Glory. A lot of people agree with you. You don't like my hair and my beard. You think I'm a tough character who goes around bullying people, and that I'm shiftless, too lazy to keep a regular job. You don't approve of me or my life-style. Well, it's your prerogative." There was no censure in his tone. It was deep and serious.

"Oh, my! Did I say all that? I had no right—it was presumptuous of me."

He glanced down at her. "You didn't have to *say* it. I could tell by the way you looked at me. But don't worry about it. You were honest enough to let your feelings show."

"I've never met anyone like you. Most of the people I've known live in a more conventional way—they're employed, or do something . . . useful."

"We're not all made in the same mold, Gloria. I don't feel the need to achieve a status in the community in order to be comfortable with myself. I depend on no one, and no one depends on me. It's as simple as that."

She waited, hoping he would keep talking and tell her something about himself, but he remained silent. It occurred to her that not once since they had taken Aunt Ethel to the hospital had she thought about his appearance. He still had the red bandana about his forehead, the long, unruly hair, and the bushy beard; but she hadn't noticed anyone at the hospital giving him so much as a second look. Why had she judged him so harshly because he didn't conform? Why was appearance so important to her? Had more of Marvin's values rubbed off on her than she realized?

Gloria loosened her hand from his, pulled his jacket more tightly about her shoulders, and moved a little away from him. The tangled lines of her thoughts emerged at one junction: She was attracted to him! The revelation both fascinated and confused her.

"I've never met anyone like you," she said again, breaking the silence.

To her relief he chuckled. "Oh, yes, you have. Have you forgotten the tough guys from the Big Windy?"

"You're not like them!"

"How do you know?"

"I just know, that's all. Now, hush up about them. Every time I think about that terrible encounter I get a nervous stomach."

"Speaking of stomachs I hope Gary left some food," he said as he turned the car into the motel drive. "I'm starved. How about you?"

"I guess I am hungry, now that you mention it. Gary must have forgotten to turn the vacancy sign on, which means we only have one guest tonight other than him and Dwight."

Jack drove past the lone car in front of unit three and pulled around to the back of the motel, where two large semitrailer trucks were parked.

"When I talked to Gary, he said he'd leave a key under the brick beside the back step, in case you didn't have one."

"I don't, unless there's one in Aunt Ethel's purse."

"Don't bother looking for it. Stay put. I'll turn on a light and come back for you and Peter." He was out of the car before Gloria thought about giving him his jacket.

The lights in the kitchen sprang on. Jack came back to lift Peter from the backseat, blankets and all, and carry him to the house. Gloria held open the door and they went inside, much like a family returning home, she thought briefly. She led the way, turning on lights as she went through the office to her room. Jack laid

105

Peter down, removed his shoes, took off his jacket, and covered him. He looked up at Gloria standing on the other side of the bed watching him.

"No argument about undressing him tonight?" he said, lifting his brows.

Her gaze met his, and she blinked. *Oh, my God, I've lost my mind. I'm really beginning to like him . . . very much.*

"Why wake him just so he can go back to sleep again?" She murmured lightly, tossing back the same words he'd used that night a week ago.

His eyes were laughing as they stared into hers. It should be a sin for a man to have such large, beautiful, expressive eyes, she thought, and turned her back to dim the light beside her son's bed. A flood of pleasure washed over her, sending excitement coursing through her veins. She was frightened by the odd fluttering in her stomach. It's hunger pangs, she told herself, just hunger pangs.

"How old is he?"

"He'll be four in a couple of weeks." She glanced over her shoulder and saw that his fingertips were combing the dark hair back from Peter's forehead. A wave of tenderness for this big, gentle man flooded her heart.

"He's a fine boy," he said softly.

Gloria went to the foot of the bed and turned to look at him. "He's had to endure more than his share of difficulties for one so young."

"He seems well adjusted and . . . happy."

"He is now. It's not always been that way."

"And you?" He was looking at her with those great,

knowing eyes while his fingertips continued to caress the child's head.

"Me too. I like it here." She said it almost defensively.

"You've had a few bad breaks, too, huh?"

"A few. But I like to think they've made me a stronger person." Her voice was shaky, and she felt a tingly sensation travel up her spine.

He nodded solemnly. "Peter's lucky he's got you."

Gloria stood glued to the floor, incapable of replying. There was a tightness across her chest, a fullness in her throat, and she couldn't utter a word. She stood there until he came toward her, then she moved ahead of him to the door.

The expression on her face hurt him deep inside. She had lowered her lashes and bitten her bottom lip, a sure sign of distress. Had her ex-husband rejected her for another woman? Was she still in love with him? It was amazing how disturbing the thought was; he didn't want her upset by anything or anyone.

Jack followed her out the door and through the office to the kitchen. There was evidence that Gary and Dwight had eaten at the kitchen table, although they had put the dirty dishes in the dishwasher.

"There's roast and potatoes." Gloria stood before the open refrigerator. "Sit down and I'll warm them up for you."

"No. You sit down and I'll fix something for you."

He was standing behind her, his hands lightly grazing her arms. A shiver of pure physical awareness ran down her spine. She was blatantly aware that this was the first time in her life she had ever experienced such primitive sexual feelings for a man. She resisted the urge to lean back, rest against him, and take comfort in his strength.

"You've done so much. The least I can do is feed—"

His hand slid beneath her arms and he casually lifted her out of the way. "Sit, Glory, before I put you in that chair and tie you there with a dish towel," he commanded gently.

She sat down, propped her elbows on the table, and rested her chin in her palms. Fatigue washed over her. The thoughts in her mind tumbled over each other in riotous confusion.

"Nothing is for sure, is it?" she said wearily. "I thought I had the tangles in my life sorted out. Now I feel like I've been run over with a steamroller." She hadn't realized she had spoken aloud until Jack answered her.

"You've just had an especially bad day. Had Ethel said anything to you about not feeling well?"

"No. But I knew she didn't, so I mentioned that she should go to the doctor for a checkup; but she was reluctant to go. I was going to try to get her there when I took Peter in for shots. What are you doing?"

"I'm making a cup of chocolate for you to drink while I fix you the best hot beef sandwich you ever ate. Just wait until—" He stopped when he saw the tears rolling down her cheeks. She was crying soundlessly. "Glory, Glory . . ."

Great sobs welled up from her throat and shuddered through her. His thoughtful concern had been the final blow to the protective shield she had wrapped around herself.

Jack came to the table, set the steaming cup in front of her, and knelt down. With a soft groan he slid his fingers into her hair and pulled her head against him. He caressed the nape of her neck with gentle finger-tips.

"Let it out, honey. Let it all out. Cry, my sweet, and then we'll talk about it." He held her close, waiting for the storm of tears to run itself dry.

"It's just hit me, Jack. Aunt Ethel will ne-ver come back to this kit-chen."

"You're thinking the worst, Glory, Glory." Her cheek was pressed to his denim shirt and she pressed her face against him.

"All I can give her is my love, my support. She has no one but me." Her voice was muffled.

"She has you and Gary, and I'll . . . be around."

"I don't know if I can do it, Jack. I just don't know," she blurted.

"You don't know what, Glory?"

"I don't know if I can keep this place running. She'll need money if she goes to a nursing home."

"Don't borrow trouble, pretty girl. She may have insurance and a nice little nest egg laid away."

"She doesn't," she said stubbornly.

"Don't worry about it now. Drink the chocolate while I fix a sandwich. Then you're off to bed. I'll sleep on Ethel's couch tonight."

"You ca-n't. You're too . . . big. Take one of the rooms."

"We'll see. C'mon. Drink up."

Gloria drank from the cup, waging a constant battle with tears that threatened to spill down her cheeks. She was suddenly aware of how she had let herself go in front of this man and how comfortable she felt lean-ing against him and confessing her fears. In all the five years she had been married to Marvin she had never allowed him to see her shed one tear.

Jack talked while he prepared the meal. "I'll get Gary to help me drag some dead trees down out of the hills, and I'll tackle that woodpile. You'll need fireplace wood and—"

"Aunt Ethel said the chain saw was broken."

"I'll bring mine down. I saw some downed oak out back. Oak makes the best firewood. Burns longer." He took toast from the toaster and put it on a plate. "I'll check the water pipes and be sure the heat tapes are working. We don't want a freeze-up."

"Heat tapes? What's that? There's so much I don't know about running this place that it scares me."

"Don't worry about it. What I don't know, Gary will." He set a plate in front of her and picked up her empty cup. "How about more chocolate?"

"No, thank you."

He fixed a plate for himself and they ate in silence. When they had finished, Jack put the dishes in the dishwasher and started the machine.

"Go to bed, Glory. I'll bunk down here on the couch, and in the morning we'll go back to the hospital."

"You don't have to go. I can take the pickup."

"We'll talk about it in the morning," he said, and gave her a gentle push toward her room. "Go to bed."

During the week that followed, Jack spent every day at the motel and every night that Gary was not there. He fixed Gloria's car so she didn't have to drive the truck, and stayed with Peter while she went to the hospital to visit her aunt. He took care of winterizing

110

the motel, things Gloria didn't even know about, cut up a supply of wood, put on the storm windows, and cleaned out the eave troughs. If she was late getting back to the motel, he started the evening meal.

Gloria was grateful for his help, but scolded herself when she realized how much she had come to depend upon him. She shouldn't allow herself to rely on this man, or any man, she told herself crossly; he would come to expect something in return. But, she reasoned, he hasn't as much as touched my hand since the night we came back from the hospital.

The doctors assured Gloria that Ethel's condition was not life threatening at the moment, although she was paralyzed on the right side and could not speak.

"We're not getting many tourists," she told her aunt one day. "Jack says people are afraid to venture off the beaten track in case the weather turns bad. He said for me to tell you he drained the water pipes going to the campground and to the end units at the motel; he turned off the heat and the electricity to those units. Jack's been a big help; I don't know what I'd have done without him. Peter thinks he gets up every morning and hangs out the sun," she said with a small laugh.

"Gary would like for his girlfriend Janet to come out and stay with me for a while," she contrived. "He says she's between jobs. I said I'd have to ask you. Is it okay?" Ethel squeezed her hand. "You've met her? And liked her? I'm glad. Gary seems to think a lot of her. He said she's a teacher, but she lost her contract when the school system had to cut back due to less federal aid."

At the end of the second week Gloria was told by

the doctors that her aunt could be moved to a nursing home. She returned to the motel with a long face.

"Oh, Jack. I wish I could take care of her here. She cried when the doctor told her she couldn't come home."

"She needs therapy you can't give her, pretty girl. Maybe in a few months she'll be well enough to come home." Jack was sitting in the rocking chair in front of the fireplace with Peter on his lap. The weather had turned surprisingly cold, and Gloria stood with her hands behind her and her back to the fire.

"I know, but I wish I could take care of her. I promised her I'd come to see her as often as I can."

"You can't make the trip alone when the weather gets bad. Your car is too light; you could slide off the road. Peter and I will take you in my four-wheel drive, won't we, Pete?"

"Gary said Janet will move out here tomorrow. She'll be here to stay with Peter."

They stared at each other for a long moment, and Gloria wondered what he was thinking. At times he pulled a mask over his emotions, and she had the feeling he was about to walk out and never come back. The thought ravaged her, sending a shiver of dread down her spine. A feeling of misery and loneliness washed over her. She stared into his eyes and asked herself how things could have developed to such a point that she would care if she ever saw him again or not. Where was her painfully acquired resolve to not get emotionally involved with any man, much less a man like Jack Evans?

Peter moved up in Jack's arms and combed his

short, stubby fingers through his beard. "I'm gonna stay with Jack. I love Jack."

Small arms wrapped themselves around Jack's neck and he looked up at Gloria, his eyes not veiled anymore. She saw such pain, anxiety, love, tenderness, and compassion in those deep, beautiful green eyes that she had an almost uncontrollable impulse to hold his shaggy head to her breast and comfort him. He held her with his eyes. She stood clenching her hands behind her while her cheeks reddened under his steady gaze. A bewildering complex of thoughts, each fleeting, merging into one another, filled her mind until one managed to stick. *Peter was becoming too attached to him.* Peter? Oh, God! What about herself? Her heart shook with apprehension. She was dangerously tempting fate. She knew it, but she couldn't do a thing about it.

"We'll have two truckers for dinner tonight. I put a meat loaf in the oven," Jack said, breaking her train of thought. "I found a recipe in Ethel's cookbook."

"I could smell it the minute I came in. I'll put some potatoes in the microwave." Anxious to break the connection that pulsed so powerfully between them, Gloria escaped to the kitchen.

CHAPTER SEVEN

"You think the boy is getting too attached to me."

Gloria glanced over her shoulder as she placed the plates in the dishwasher. Jack was standing beside the kitchen table, his hands on the knobs of the high-backed chair.

After the meal Peter had insisted that Jack put him to bed. Gloria, with a small frown creasing her brows, had watched him sweep the small boy up into his arms. The frown hadn't escaped Jack's watchful eyes.

"I . . . don't want him disappointed."

"Do you think I'd do that?"

"Not intentionally." Gloria rinsed the silverware in the sink and arranged it in the basket in the dishwasher. "He doesn't understand—"

"That I'm not a permanent fixture in his life."

"Something like that."

"Do you want me to stay away from the boy?"

"No!" The cry of protest came straight from her heart. She was on the verge of tears and blinked rapidly. "It . . . would break his heart. He looks forward to each day because of you."

"I don't want you to worry about me ever doing anything to upset you . . . or Peter. He's a smart little fellow, a fine boy—a boy any man would be proud of," he said softly.

Not *any* man. The words were a silent scream filling her mind. Gloria swallowed hard, fighting back the tears. Marvin wasn't proud of Peter. Marvin couldn't stand to look at him; he thought of him as a stray to be fed and patted on the head occasionally, not a real person with feelings. But that was in the past. She didn't want to think about it and hurried to rally her thoughts.

"He's been happy here. It's mostly because of you."

"What about you, Glory? Have you been happy here?"

She made herself look him directly in the eyes. Hers were wet, her vision blurred. "Yes. It's such a relief to be able to be . . . myself."

They stared at each other for a moment that was so still, it was as though time had stopped moving. Then, slowly and haltingly, Jack came to her and stood towering over her. He held out his hand. The gesture caught her off guard, and she looked at him searchingly before putting her hand in his.

"I know the feeling." The words came out as if it was a relief to say them. Still holding her hand he reached for the light switch and shut it off, plunging the room into semidarkness. "Come sit with me for a while," he invited softly. He steered her to the couch; she would have preferred the rocking chair. "Shall we see what's on?" He knelt down in front of the television and turned it on. The movie that came on was an old John Wayne western she'd seen several times before.

"Is this okay?"

"Fine."

He sat down beside her, reached for her hand, and engulfed it in his. He stretched his long legs out in front of him, his head resting on the back of the couch.

"This is nice." He let out a half sigh, half yawn. "I like the peace and quiet, the companionship, the . . . just being here with you. I didn't realize how lonely my life had become until I met you and Peter."

She glanced at him. His head was turned toward her and his green eyes held hers like a magnet. There was a sense of unreality in having him here, sharing in the preparation of the meal, taking Peter to bed together, sitting with him during the quiet of the evening. The careful way he had pushed her down onto the couch, his soft, sincere words, the touch of his hand holding hers, called out to something deep inside of her, brought her emotions to the brink of exploding. Ten seconds passed while Gloria drew a shallow breath, followed by a deeper one. She shook her head as if in answer to a question.

"You think I want to make love to you. Is that it?" The question was delivered suddenly.

"No, I just think . . ." She continued to shake her head. Her heart began to beat heavily.

"You're wrong. I want to . . . very much. I've wanted to since the first time I saw you. Since the very first," he whispered once more, his face near hers, his hands drawing her to him. "I doubt if there's a man alive who wouldn't want to make love to you if he were here with you like this."

Oh, yes, there is, she thought. *But a man like you wouldn't understand that. He looks tired,* she thought; *he has shadows beneath his eyes. Has he been working*

116

too hard, not sleeping well? She felt warmth sweeping over her. *Oh, God! What if he can read my mind?* Her breath caught in the back of her throat, but when she spoke, she chose her tone carefully.

"You'd never force me."

He lifted her hand, gently disengaged her fingers from around his, and held it tightly between his two palms. He looked at it intently, then brought her fingers to his mouth and gently brushed his lips across her knuckles.

"No. I'd never do that." He placed her hand, palm up, in his. "Such a little hand." He spoke as if he were talking to himself. "I like it." He turned his head toward her. "I like everything about you, Glory."

She didn't move. She felt her insides warm with pleasure as she looked into the quiet face and soft green eyes now anxiously waiting to see if she would take his admission lightly and throw back a sassy retort. Love and tenderness welled within her. She lifted her free hand and held it to his cheek. Still holding her eyes with his he turned his lips into her palm. She felt them move, felt the warmth of his breath. There had been no games between them, no sassy retorts, no pretense, since the night they had taken her aunt to the hospital. He had offered her his help, his friendship, openly and honestly, with no strings attached. Suddenly all the emotional bruising she'd had to endure from Marvin flowed and melted away under the serious but tender look in his eyes.

"There's a lot I like about you, too, Jack." She was so absorbed in her own thoughts that it was seconds, or minutes, before she realized that his eyes were no longer serious. They were twinkling.

"In spite of the beard?"

"And the hair . . . and the earring. . . ."

His hand went to his ear and he tugged. "I don't know how you women wear such things. It hurt like hell!"

"It serves you right for trying to aggravate me."

He gazed at her for a long moment before he reached out a hand to stroke a finger down her cheek with a feather-light touch. Her thoughts shifted to how absolutely masculine he was, how capable he was of doing anything he wanted to do. He would have made a wonderful pioneer, a man who would have blazed a trail into the wilderness, built a cabin with his own hands, taken care of his woman—

"Have you ever kissed a man with a beard?"

"Thousands."

He growled fiercely, and his long arms reached out to envelop her and lock her to him. "How about making it a thousand and one?"

Gloria heard herself, amazingly, laughing. She turned her head from side to side, until his fingers cupped her chin. The eyes that smiled into his were glittering pools of molten gold.

"Aha!" she cried. "Now your caveman character comes out!"

"I don't think you realize what a sweet invitation you are, sitting there with your eyes shining and your soft mouth smiling. I've wanted to kiss you from the first minute I saw you," he said huskily, and lowered his mouth to hers. His lips were soft and gentle. The brush of his beard caressed her face and was surprisingly pleasant. "Everything about you turns me on, in spite of all I can do to resist you. This little upper lip of yours—this little crease beside your mouth that's caused by pressing your lips together to keep from smiling." He licked it with his tongue. "You're going to have smile lines here." His lips touched the corners of her eyes. "And when you're older, and your hair is twisted in a knot on the top of your head, you'll be even more beautiful than you are now." Her lids fluttered down. "Open your eyes, Glory, Glory, and look at me."

"Jack, I don't sleep around." She raised gold-tipped lashes and immediately became lost in the clear-green pools of his eyes.

"I know that. Put your arms around me, Glory," he whispered. Warm fingers smoothed her hair away from her face and then cupped the back of her head.

Mindless, unconscious of time or place, she lifted her arms and encircled his neck in complete disregard of the common sense that told her she was acting wantonly, unrestrainedly, and foolishly. She leaned back to look into his eyes.

"You have beautiful eyes, Jack."

"Yours are like those I've seen on a beautiful little mountain lion—wide, questioning, soft, but fierce too." His arms tightened and his lips nuzzled her ear. They felt so good, she pressed against them.

"I scratch too."

"Nooo." He drew the word out. "You purr. You're a delicious armful, Glory, Glory. I've wanted to kiss you with your arms around my neck, your breasts pressed against me, and your hips in my hands for . . . oh, so long. But I won't do it, if you tell me to stop. Are you going to?"

"I should. . . ."

A wild, sweet enchantment rippled through her veins as his mouth moved over hers with warm urgency. The desire to push her fingers through his hair was an impulse she couldn't resist. It was so thick and so soft, like the mustache and beard that swept across her face. His kiss deepened and her head began to spin helplessly from the torrent of churning desires racking her body. The intensity of these feelings was strange to her, but she was not frightened by them. The sensations were heightened when his tongue caressed her lips, sought entrance, and found welcome. When she felt his mouth leaving hers, she held the back of his head with her hand more tightly. Finally, reluctantly, they broke the kiss so they could breathe.

"Glory, sweet one . . . I shouldn't have started this! You're so soft to touch, so sweet to taste, and you smell so womanly." He gently pulled her over onto him, and his hand moved down her back to her hips. He cupped them and pressed her to his male hardness; arousing her, taking her over, making her want the physical gratification of uniting with him in the most intimate way. "Tell me to stop . . . to go home—or it'll be too late." The words seemed to be wrenched from him. "I . . . ache for you. . . ."

Caught in a spinning whirlwind of desire Gloria was aware that his pulse was racing as wildly as hers. She was causing this! His virile, vitally strong body was reacting to hers! It was something she'd never experienced with Marvin. Stirred by this incredible discovery she met his passion with intimate sensuousness and parted her lips to run the tip of her tongue across his mouth.

"God! Sweetheart . . . help me to stop this . . . while I still can!"

"No!" Her chin tilted almost fearlessly, as joyous thoughts whirled and flitted through her mind. *I'm doing what I want, for once. This is dangerous, but it could very well be the most precious moment of my life!*

She moved her hips against him in an instinctive invitation as old as time. Finding what her body had craved for so long, Gloria ignored the warning signals flashing in her brain and allowed the warmth of his desire and tenderness to wash over her. The world could be ending the next minute and her only concern would be to stay with him, relieve them both of the trembling hunger bedeviling them.

"Don't tease me, Glory!" he whispered hoarsely. His lips ravaged her face from cheek to chin. "Night after lonely night I've thought about being with you like this."

"I'm not teasing. . . ." she moaned desperately, her face flaming with shame.

"It's everything or nothing! Say it, now, while I can still leave you!" he said raggedly.

She burrowed her face into the softness of his beard. "Don't leave me," she whispered, her voice anxious. "Love me, Jack."

"You're sure?"

"Please!"

Her plea seemed to act as a potent aphrodisiac. His body responded with violent trembling. He pulled her roughly against his hard arousal, as if to leave her no doubt that he was desperate for her. "Oh, sweet one . . ."

Jack stood and lifted her in his arms. A half-dozen

121

strides brought him to Ethel's bedroom. The only light in the room was what came through the open doorway from the living room. He stood her on her feet and put his arms around her. They stood for a long moment, arms wrapped around each other, close, savoring the feel of standing for the first time in each other's arms. His face was against the top of her head, hers in the curve of his neck.

"I'm afraid to leave you," he muttered thickly. "I'm afraid you'll not be here when I come back. Sweetheart . . . sweet, sweet girl . . . I must go lock the door, turn off the TV, and the vacancy light—"

"I'll be here. Hurry."

He left her, and she turned her back to the door. Her eyes were wide open, staring at nothing. Her mind grappled, not with what she was doing, but with her lack of sexual experience and the violence of her own need for him to make love to her. She had experienced nothing but humiliation at the hands of her husband, and her female heart cried out to know if that was all there was. *Please, God, show me that what happens between a man and a woman can be beautiful.*

It seemed to her she had stood there for an eternity before arms encircled her from behind, and warm lips and a soft beard nuzzled the sensitive spot below her ear. His hands moved to cup her breasts, squeezing them gently.

"You're the most utterly feminine woman I've ever met." Gloria closed her eyes and let the soft purr of his voice and the feel of his hands consume her. "You've bewitched me. I seem to have lost control where you're concerned."

"Oh, Jack . . ." His persuasive whisper, the touch

of his hands, called out to a deep need inside her, and the explosion of sensation choked off her voice.

"My head says stay away from you, but my hands want to know every soft curve of your body." He moved his hand down to pull her tightly back against him. "Glory, Glory, come quench this thirst I have for you!"

When she didn't answer, or move, he backed up a step with her in his arms, sat down on Ethel's bed, and pulled her onto his lap. She clung to his shoulders, which were wide and powerful and sheltering. The feel of his body, the stroking of his hands, the warm moistness of his breath, and the love spilling from her heart erased the last shred of her inhibitions, and with a soft cry she gave herself up to the sweet abandonment he was urging upon her, telling herself that no matter what happened in the morning, she could face it if she had this night to remember always.

Their mouths met and were no longer gentle. They kissed deeply, hungrily. His hand found her breast, cupped and lifted it. Her own fingers curled feverishly into the solid muscle of his back, and her lips ravaged his neck. When his fingers moved to the front zipper of her jeans her hand went automatically to his and he stopped immediately.

"Do you have doubts?" he moaned hoarsely against her cheek.

"No . . . no. . . ." Her hand caressed his silky beard. "It's just . . . I'm afraid you'll think I'm . . . easy."

A low protest came from his throat. "Easy? Oh, God, no! You're anything but that. I'm thinking you're so small, so perfect, so beautiful—I get the feeling you've not done this before . . . yet I know you have. But I don't want to think of it, or for you to think of it. I want you to think I'm your first, that you're mine alone," he murmured.

She felt a sweetness, a rightness, when he lowered her to the bed and stretched out beside her. She gave a shiver of pure pleasure when he unbuttoned her shirt and slipped it off her shoulders. Slowly he tugged her jeans down over her hips, but left her panties in place. When he left her to take off his clothes, she lifted the covers and moved between the sheets.

She wasn't prepared for the warmth or the strength of his hard, muscular body, the long, hairy legs against her, the enormous arms under and around her. Her trembling body was gathered tenderly to a warm, naked chest thickly matted with soft hair.

"Sweetheart . . ." He smoothed her hair back from her face. Even now his concern was for her, and she cherished it.

"I can't believe I'm here with you, like this." Even as she spoke, her hands clutched him closer, her stomach muscles tightened, her breathing and heartbeat were all mixed up. *I love him,* she thought wildly. *I wouldn't be here in bed with him if I didn't love him. Oh, dear heaven! It's happened so fast. It's unreal that I'm doing this, feeling this.*

"Glory, Glory. You're every sweet dream I've ever dreamed, every fantasy." His hungry mouth searched, found hers, and held it with fierce but tender possession. His hands moved urgently over her, and she felt as if her heart would gallop right out of her breast.

She wanted to speak, to tell him she was still a girl in a woman's body, that she was afraid of the hurt that would follow this giving of herself. She opened her mouth to voice her fears, but it was too late. He covered her parted lips, his tongue darting hotly in and out of her mouth, exploring every curve of the sweetness that trembled beneath his demanding kiss. She moaned gently and panted for breath.

"Are you shy with me?" he whispered between kisses. "Don't be. I'll not do anything you don't want me to do. You're beautiful. Your little body is tight and neat. Your skin is soft—like velvet. . . ." His fingers fumbled with the hooks on her bra, then swept it from her breasts. He nuzzled them gently, kissed them reverently, and then for the first time she experienced having her nipples pressed to a man's lips. His hand pushed at her panties and she lifted her hips to help him.

So this is what it's like to really make love with a man, she thought dreamily, and threaded her legs between his. His sex was large and firm and throbbed against her stomach. She gloried in the feel of him, knowing that soon he could fill that aching emptiness. Her hands moved over his ribs and sides, down over his back to his hips.

He kissed her breast; his tongue flicked the bud, then he grasped it gently with his teeth. The softness of his beard was a silky caress on her stomach. Tremors shot through her with earth-shaking waves as his exploring fingers moved over her body, prowling ever closer to the ultimate goal. Suddenly they were *there,* sliding into the mysterious moistness. She welcomed the gentle probing with parted thighs and an urgency that incited him to lift his mouth to hers in a kiss that stripped away everything but the need to assuage the ache building to unbearable heights within her. He slid smoothly over her body and she welcomed the weight that pressed onto her.

"Now? Little sweet one . . . now?" he murmured, and sought entrance while she waited in rapt and aching anguish. She pressed herself to him, her arms winding tightly around his neck. She was caught up in overpowering desire and the need for physical release. "Oh, Lord! You're so small, so tight. Will I hurt you?" His chest heaved as he attempted to control his breathing.

"You won't hurt me, darling. Don't stop!" she pleaded, her need for him overcoming her shyness. Her hands feverishly clung to him, holding him tightly while she rained fervent kisses on his mouth.

He raised his head, his eyes searching her passion-clouded ones, and then with a muttered whisper he closed his arms about her in fierce demand. He moved into her, reverently guiding her to accept the gently rhythmic sliding. This joining would be forever imprinted in her memory. She was part of this man. He was the universe, vibrating with all the love in the world, and he was lifting her to undreamed of sensual heights, reaching, reaching. . . .

He supported himself on his forearms, tangled his hands in her hair. "I wanted our first time to be long and sweet . . . but, darling . . . I can't wait much longer!"

"You . . . don't have to wait. . . ." She arched to impale herself more completely on his throbbing warmth.

"Oh, God! Oh, love—" He probed urgently, turning this way and that, and moaned with pleasure.

Gloria desperately wanted what they were reaching for, dreaded missing it, and quivered with expectation beneath the pressure of his body. She clung to him, aware only of that thrusting, pulsing rhythm increasing unbearably to a tempo that brought her higher . . . higher—

She came languidly back to reality and found her hands clasping Jack's tight buttocks, his bearded face pressed to her neck. He was still huge and deep inside her, but the waves of frenzied pleasure that had ripped through her were subsiding. In their place swelled a burning desire to comfort and pleasure him. Her hands moved lovingly over him, smoothed his hair back from his face, stroked it, hugged his head to her breast. With utmost tenderness she pressed her lips to his forehead. She had learned the mysteries about which she had read and imagined, but which she'd never truly believed were accompanied by such overwhelmingly forceful feelings. It was almost as if they were totally and completely in love!

He was a stranger to her, his background as different from hers as night from day, she thought frantically. And yet she felt as though she'd known him all her life, wanted him, needed him, loved him.

His heart was still thundering against hers when he wrapped his legs around her and turned on his side, taking her with him. They lay quietly facing each other, her soft belly tight against his hard one. They kissed for a long time, as if it were the first time and there never could be anything beyond a kiss. His tongue was inside her mouth and moving softly and slowly while his fingers teased the nipple on her breast and then drifted lightly down to her belly and fluttered their way to the place where they were joined. The varieties of stroking thrilled her in a thousand different ways, creating a hunger deep, deep inside her. She knew she should be shocked, but she wasn't. The feeling was so acutely pleasurable that she tightened her arms and legs about him and murmured unintelligible words in his ear. He laughed deep in his throat. It was a tender, loving, knowing laugh.

"I wish I could see your eyes. You're so incredibly sweet, Glory, Glory. I want you to feel everything—"

"I'll explode—" She arched against him when he flexed his hips. "Jack . . ."

"Talk to me, darling. Tell me what you want, what you feel. I've never known anything more wonderful than the feel of you tight against me, surrounding me. You're like a warm, living china doll—sweet, fragile, yet strong, passionate. Oh, be still, darling!" he breathed in gasps when she moved urgently. Then, "Yes! Oh, yes!" With a long breath he thrust at her full force, and incredibly her body responded to his. They merged into a long, long, unbelievably beautiful release and lay shuddering in each other's arms.

Gloria held him tenderly. She felt an odd sense of power. This big, rough man had quivered in her arms as she had in his. He had made her feel as if she were wonderful, precious, worthwhile—they had come together, as equals, in dignity and need. Slowly his breathing steadied, and he rolled onto his back. His arms pulled her to him and his hand sought her thigh to bring it up to rest on his. They were quiet for a long while, her head on his shoulder, his hand stroking her thigh.

"This brings a new dimension to our relationship," he said softly.

Gloria held her breath through the seconds of silence that followed. She looked up. The face that was so close to hers was not smiling—she could see clearly enough for that.

"Oh, there's no need for you to feel obligated," she said, trying to keep the quiver out of her voice.

"Obligated? What the hell are you talking about?"

"I don't want you to think . . . that I expect—"

"Hush!" The word was sharp, and there wasn't a trace of humor in his voice.

Gloria peered at him apprehensively, trying to read his expression. A few seconds ago she had felt young and happy and cherished, and she wanted desperately to feel again that closeness of mind and body they'd shared.

Jack turned his head toward her. "You're not just a one-night stand. There's much more between us than that. We've got to get it all sorted out."

She shut her eyes tightly to hold back the tears. *Don't spoil it,* she cautioned. *Don't let him know how afraid you are of being alone, or how much his tenderness means to you.* Their union had been everything she had dreamed a union between a man and a woman in love would be. But he had not said anything to her about love. . . .

"I can't leave Peter in there by himself. He might wake up and be frightened." She threw back the sheet covering them. Jack's arms tightened around her, refusing to let her go.

"I thought about that. I'll bring him in to sleep on the couch where we can hear him if he wakes up."

129

"No. I'll go."

"Don't go. Stay here with me, Glory. Let me sleep with you in my arms. You keep all my ghosts at bay, my sweet one." His voice was husky and pleading, and tore at her heart. "Say you'll stay."

"All right," she said mindlessly.

"I'll get Peter."

When he was gone, her hands sought the warm spot where his body had lain. *Oh, dear Lord! I've gotten myself in deep trouble this time. I've fallen in love with an aging hippie!* she thought miserably. *He's sweet and kind, but there's nothing else about him that I admire. He has no ambition. He's content with his hand-to-mouth existence in an old shack in the mountains, and he's ruthless when crossed. I could never live the way he lives, especially with Peter—I need security. Besides, I know absolutely nothing about his background. He could have a criminal record, or be married, for all I know. And what would my family think if I came riding up to the house on a motorcycle with a man with long hair and a beard? They'd be sure, then, that I'd lost my mind.*

Something he'd muttered in her ear while in the throes of passion came filtering into her mind. *I want our first time to be long and sweet.* Did he plan for this to be a regular arrangement—that they would perform a service for each other? Dear God! Did he think she was the type of woman who would enter into such a relationship?

Such thoughts ran wildly through her mind as she stared into the darkness, but when Jack returned, slipped into bed beside her, and gathered her tenderly to him, she went to him eagerly and nestled against his strength. In spite of all the reasons she'd cited against continuing a relationship with this big, rugged, sometimes fierce man—he made her feel wanted and . . . safe.

Long after Jack had fallen into a deep sleep, Gloria lay cozily against his very male body. No one could doubt *his* fundamental virility—it radiated from every pore in his aggressively masculine body. She pushed the thought of the *other* sexual experience she'd had out of her mind. Jack's lovemaking had been tumultuous, and she had responded vigorously to his instruction in the elementary pleasures of loving.

As far as she was concerned, he was her first and only *real* lover.

CHAPTER EIGHT

Morning came, and with it the realization that she was alone in Ethel's bed. The bedroom door was closed, but she could hear the sound of voices coming from the living room—Gary's, Jack's, and Peter's. The clock on the bedside table was turned face down. She turned it up and was astonished to see that it was nine o'clock. Heavens! She hadn't slept that late in ages.

She threw back the covers, and the cold air hit her naked body, giving her goose bumps. There was a soreness and a stickiness between her legs. She grabbed her clothes and went into the bathroom, carefully locking the door behind her. The face that looked back at her from the mirror was the same face she'd seen yesterday morning. How could that be, when she felt so different inside? A man had made love to her all through the night—a tender, caring, considerate man, a man as different from her former husband as day from night. Marvin had cruelly, and hurtfully, taken her virginity, leaving no doubt that it was distasteful to him to do so, but that duty was duty and *legally* he was required to consummate the marriage; then he had left their bed on their wedding night, never to return. Jack had made sure that she shared in the enjoyment of their union, kissed away her tears when heightened emotion caused them to spill from her eyes, held her in his arms while she slept.

Gloria stepped into the shower and let the warm water splash over her. She wondered with increasing anxiety what Jack's attitude toward her would be this morning. Would he be flippant about what happened between them? Would he simply ignore it? Had it meant anything to him, beyond physical relief? Would he take it for granted that he was welcome in her bed for as long as he wanted her?

She washed herself quickly, dressed, then combed her short blond hair into place. No use in prolonging the agony, she told herself. Face him and get it over with.

She found Gary alone in the kitchen; he was getting ready to go out the back door.

"Morning. I heard Peter. Did he go back to our room?"

"Jack took him up to his place. He said to let you sleep. He thinks you've about wore yourself out."

"I . . . was tired." She turned to pour a cup of coffee, because she could feel her cheeks tingle.

"I'm on my way to get Janet. She'll be a big help to you."

"She can have Aunt Ethel's room. I'll get it ready."

"No way," Gary said with an earthy laugh. "That woman's stayin' with me!"

"Oh! Of course. Um . . . Gary, did Jack say when he'd be back?"

"No. He just said tell you he had Peter with him. Don't worry about the kid. Jack'll take care of him."

"I know that. I was just wondering—"

133

"I'll stop and see Ethel. I should be back by noon, and then you can go."

Gloria stood at the sink and watched Gary back his station wagon out of the garage. She gulped down the coffee, then gathered up her cleaning supplies and started her rounds. Work was the only thing that would keep her thoughts at bay this morning.

Gary returned with Janet shortly after noon. She was a short, full-figured woman with shoulder-length dark hair and soft, dark eyes. Gloria liked her immediately; she was warm and friendly, and obviously very much in love with Gary. She made fresh coffee while Gloria made sandwiches. The three of them sat at the kitchen table and talked about Ethel and the motel until the clock struck two.

"I thought Peter would be back by now," Gloria remarked anxiously.

"Are you going to see Ethel today? I told her you'd probably come this afternoon," Gary said.

"I was, but I hate to go not knowing about Peter."

"Janet and I will be here. We'll look after him if Jack comes back and wants to leave again—which I doubt." Gary grinned and winked at Janet.

The realization hit Gloria like a dash of cold water that Gary knew she and Jack had spent the night in Ethel's room. *Well, so what?* she thought stubbornly. *I'm an adult, and I don't feel one bit guilty.* Yet, despite her determination to handle herself coolly in this new situation she found herself in, she was frightened, anxious, and apprehensive about seeing Jack again.

"If you're sure you don't mind looking after Peter, I'll go on to town. I want to get back before dark."

"Don't worry about a thing." Janet got up to clear the table. "I'm here to help."

Jack had brought Peter back to the motel while she was in town, and left again before she returned. Peter chattered endlessly about the day: about his dog, watching a jackrabbit run, seeing kittens, a covey of quail, a pocket gopher, a badger. The small boy was so full of what all he'd seen and heard, the words tumbled over each other as they spilled out of his small mouth.

"Jack's dog's name's Ringo. It's big and black and has a short tail. Jack makes him mind. He yells and Ringo walks beside him. Guess what, Mom? Jack's town is old . . . the streets are all dirt. . . . Jack let me dig in the street—"

Jack, Jack, Jack. Peter had said his name a hundred times since coming home. It was hours after his usual bedtime that he calmed down enough to go to sleep. Gloria sat beside him for a long while before she got into her own bed.

"Oh, Jack," she whispered into the silent room. "Thank you for giving my son such a wonderful day." Almost without knowing it she added, "And me such a wonderful night."

Gloria thought about her visit earlier that day with her Aunt Ethel. She had been pleased to see how well her aunt was adjusting to the home. She was in a wheelchair now, and there was always someone willing to take her out into the main room where there were a television and a pool table, and where numerous card games were going on almost all day. Gradually she was getting her speech back and no longer cried when Gloria had to leave. Her eyes sparkled when Gloria told her Janet and Gary were going to be married, and that they planned to stay at the motel until they found a house so they could have Gary's little girl with them.

"Good . . . good . . . but you?" Ethel had asked her with an anxious look in her eyes.

"Don't worry about me. Peter and I will keep the motel going until you can come home. I have an income from Marvin." Gloria knew the white lie was necessary. It wouldn't do at all for her aunt to know she'd cut herself off from Marvin's money when she left Ohio, and that all she had was her small personal savings and a little money from the sale of a few pieces of jewelry he'd given her.

The days passed slowly until a week had gone by, with no sign of Jack. Gloria became increasingly sure that he was deliberately staying away to convey the message that he wanted no deep or lasting relationship with her. She was angry at herself for thinking about him, and angry at him for presuming she wanted a relationship with him.

She had promised herself she could handle whatever came up as the result of this impulsive trip west, and so far she had, even Aunt Ethel's illness. Now it was time to take another step, and she had done so. She'd sent out queries about job opportunities in Great Falls. She had decided that if Ethel sold the motel she would move on.

After a morning visit to the nursing home she stopped at the grocery store for a few things, and at the ten-cent store she got a new coloring book for Peter. The air was cold and damp, and dark clouds rolled out of the northwest. The smell of woodsmoke, hanging low, greeted her when she turned into the drive. She parked the car and hurried into the living quarters of the motel.

Janet was putting a load of sheets and towels in the washer when Gloria came in the back door with her arms filled with sacks.

"Wow! You must've bought out the town."

"Not quite. But I did get the makings for a yummy cake, a couple boxes of cereal for Peter, and a new coloring book."

"Yummy cake? Sounds good . . . and fattening."

"It is good, and loaded with calories, but what the heck. You melt caramels and add chocolate chips and coconut for the filling of a chocolate cake. I'll copy the recipe for you."

"I'd like that. Gary loves desserts." Janet added soap to the machine and turned the dial to start it. "Jack was here while you were gone. He took Peter back home with him. I didn't think you'd mind."

Gloria turned quickly and started taking the groceries from the sack. "Did he say when they'd be back? It's getting terribly cold, and it could snow."

"He wasn't on the cycle. He had the Ranger, and he put Peter in his snowsuit. He'll be all right."

"Yes, of course," Gloria said absently. She put the groceries away automatically. It was clear now that he was avoiding her. But how had he known she wouldn't be here? He must have called on the CB, she reasoned, and Janet must have told him she'd gone to town. She wished she had the nerve to ask Janet.

The day moved slowly. Janet went to the room she shared with Gary. Gloria made the yummy cake and left it on the kitchen counter to cool. The stillness of the house bore down on her. She missed Peter's chatter, his endless questions. She thought of using the CB radio to call the Hangtown station. If Jack answered, she didn't know what she'd say to him besides, "What the hell do you mean coming here and taking my son?" No, she wouldn't say that. Peter had talked of nothing but Jack, and how he was going to come get him and show him the antelope that came down to the salt blocks he'd put just outside of his town.

She wouldn't chastise him for taking Peter; it would be mean to deprive Peter of his company just because she and Jack were having their problems. When she saw him again, she'd treat him the same as she had *before:* friendly, but strictly impersonal. There was no way she would let him know how crushed she was, how miserable she felt, how used. His denial of her, now, would tarnish forever the memories of the beautiful moments they'd shared.

She sat on a stool behind the counter in the office and watched the cars go by. She was deep in thought when the long, shiny black car with the tinted glass turned into the drive and stopped in front of the office door. Gloria gaped in surprise; she knew immediately who it was, and was gripped with apprehension. She got slowly to her feet and was standing when the back door of the car opened and Marvin, holding his hat with one gloved hand, stepped out.

He stood beside the car and looked the building up and down; Gloria was sure he was mentally assessing its worth, for money was forever on his mind. The wind blew open his long black overcoat, and it flapped out behind him like wings. When he reached the office door, the driver opened it for him, then went back to the car.

Marvin looked around the office haughtily, ignoring Gloria until he'd finished his survey of the premises. Then he looked at her.

"Well, Gloria, I must say you've certainly buried yourself in the sticks. Back to your roots, huh?" He removed his hat, placed it on the counter, removed his gloves, and carefully smoothed with his fingertips the silver hair at his temples. Almost colorless gray eyes looked into hers, and he lifted his arched brows disdainfully. His every word, his every gesture, was meant to intimidate.

"What do you want?" Gloria demanded angrily. She was surprised at what little effect he had on her. Where was the old fear, the feeling of inferiority, she used to experience when she was with him?

Marvin sensed her detachment and gave her the silent treatment, looking at her with narrowed eyes, mouth turned down slightly at the corners as if he smelled something unpleasant, hand poised in front of him as if ready to flick away dust or lint from his coat. The look had been cultivated and refined over the years, and usually managed to reduce even the most self-assured person into quivering servitude.

Suddenly laughter bubbled up in Gloria's throat. How could she ever have been frightened by this . . . phony? Something goaded her to say, "Stop playacting, Marvin. I've seen this act a hundred times. What do you want?"

"Be careful what you say, Gloria. I still have the means of taking from you what you treasure the most. Why you value this cheap, tawdry life-style or the company of truckers and barroom scum is beyond me, but as long as you do, I'll not hesitate to use it to my advantage."

"You'll never get your hands on Peter—not as long as I live!"

"That's up to you, entirely up to you."

"I'm not coming back to you, Marvin. I've got the right to live my own life without interference from you. Understand that right now."

"My dear girl, if it were at all possible I'd just as soon never see you or that . . . child again. But unfortunately, you made an impression on some of my friends and business associates and they have inquired about you. I simply cannot let you and my . . . *son* disappear. People will think I've cast you off. So I've come to take you back to Cincinnati."

"I'm not going!"

"Very well, stay. I'll take the boy."

"He's not *your* boy, dammit!" Her poise completely abandoned her, and she heard herself shouting.

"Control yourself. Your lack of breeding is showing."

Gloria drew in a deep, pained breath. "Don't tell me about breeding, you fatheaded stuffed shirt! I've got more breeding in my little finger than you've got in your whole body."

"Gloria, you really are a stupid girl; beautiful, but stupid." Marvin raised his brows, and his mocking eyes surveyed her face.

"You're not taking Peter! You don't even like him!"

"No, I don't. But that's beside the point. You and Peter are coming back with me. We are going to remarry and you will conduct yourself in such a manner as to not cast a blemish on the Masterson name."

"I will not marry you again!" she hissed, glaring into his cold gray eyes.

Marvin reached into the inside pocket of his overcoat and drew out a long white envelope. He opened it and unfolded a legal document.

"The court has given me custody of the boy for six months out of the year." There was a triumphant gleam in his eyes as he watched her face turn ashen. "Come back with me, take your place as Mrs. Marvin Masterson, or I take him now."

"When we got the divorce you didn't want custody. Why are you doing this?"

"If you had not run off like a silly girl, it wouldn't have been necessary."

"I don't understand you. I don't understand you at all. Why do you want us there?"

"My dear girl, I plan to run for governor, and the image I wish to project is of a devoted family man who carefully guards the welfare of his young wife and child."

"Peter and I despise you!"

His eyes narrowed with anger. "Do you think that matters to me? You carry the Masterson name."

Something in his eyes caused a feeling of panic to sweep over her. Her heart pounded, and she felt a compelling urgency to turn and run. She felt as if she were floating through space, and tried to get her scattered thoughts together. There had to be something she could do—if only she had time to think! She breathed deeply and tried to stem the tears of rage that

141

were stinging her eyelids. Vaguely she heard the back door slam.

"Mom! Mom! Look what I got. Look what Jack—" Peter's happy shout stopped abruptly when he saw Marvin.

A fierce pain pierced Gloria's heart when she saw the look of terror on the face of her small son. She knelt down beside him. "What do you have here? A kitten! Oh, Peter—it's beautiful!"

Peter moved close to her and peered over her shoulder at the man who stared at him so coldly.

"Where are your manners, boy? Get rid of that animal and step up here and shake hands as you've been taught to do. I've come to take you home. What you need is a good school where you'll not be coddled and allowed to run wild."

Peter's stricken eyes sought Gloria's. "I'm afraid we have no choice," she said softly, and hugged him.

Peter looked up at Marvin, then back to Gloria. His face crumbled and he burst into tears. The kitten became frightened and jumped out of his arms. Peter struggled to leave Gloria's embrace and she let him go.

"Jack! Jack!" he cried between sobs, and ran out of the office.

Gloria felt sick. Poor little fellow, poor little boy; he'd been so happy here. She could hear the low murmur of Jack's voice as he talked to the boy.

"Well—are you coming or not? The sooner I get out of this backwater and back to civilization, the better." Marvin folded the paper and put it back into the envelope.

"Now?"

"Now. I'll wait in the car. Be out in ten minutes."

142

"What's going on here, Gloria?" Jack came into the room and stood at the end of the counter. Peter's arms were locked tightly about his neck, and his small legs were around his waist.

Gloria's eyes flew to Marvin, and the contempt she saw on his face as he looked at Jack only ignited her anger into full-fledged rage.

"Marvin Masterson, my ex-husband, has come to take me and Peter back to Cincinnati. His image as the devoted patriarch of the Masterson dynasty, which, by the way, includes servants, ex-wives, and adopted children, slipped when Peter and I left. He can't afford to have his friends think he's anything but a loving family man." She shouted the last few words, and tears rolled down her cheeks.

"You're divorced, aren't you? He can't make you do anything you don't want to do," Jack said calmly.

"Oh, but he can! He's got a court order that gives him custody of Peter for six months out of the year. I can't let Peter go alone with him," she wailed.

"I'll wait in the car." Marvin carefully placed his hat on his head and pulled on his gloves.

"Stay here!" Jack spoke so sharply that Marvin turned to stare at him as if he couldn't quite believe this bearded, long-haired, leather-coated yokel would have the nerve to speak to him. "Take the boy," Jack said gently, and handed Peter over to Gloria. "I want to take a look at that court order."

Peter wrapped his arms about Gloria and buried his face in her neck. The agony that pierced her heart was unbearable; she longed to be out from under the sneering gaze of the man she had married when she was so young and so naive.

"I want to see the court order," Jack repeated, and held out his hand.

Marvin's cold gray eyes flicked from Jack to Gloria and back again. Disapproval etched lines between his carefully arched brows. The grim line of his jaw and his tightly pressed lips told her that he was burning with anger.

"My advice to you is—stay out of things that don't concern you." With the faintest suggestion of a sardonic sneer he turned to go out the door.

"You're beginning to annoy me. Give me the court order!" Jack put a hand on Marvin's shoulder and spun him around. He slammed him against the wall and held him there with his forearm jammed against his Adam's apple. "Give it to me or I'll break both of your goddamm legs!"

"Get your hands off me, you ruffian. I'll call my driver."

"Do that, you bastard! I'll mop up the floor with both of you."

Gloria's heart was thudding like a jackhammer in her breast. She had no doubt that Jack would do exactly what he said he'd do. Oh, God! If he beat up Marvin, it would only make matters worse.

"Jack, don't!" The words left her mouth in a whisper.

"Now, listen, you arrogant son of a bitch, I don't intend to mess around with you. I mean to see that court order before you leave here. Give it to me, or I'll take it." Jack punctuated his words by slamming Marvin's head back against the wall.

"Ah . . . ah . . . all right." Marvin reached into his pocket for the envelope.

Jack snatched it out of his hand. "Stay right there," he snarled when Marvin started to move away from him.

Marvin straightened his hat and threw Gloria a furious glance. "You'll hear from my attorney," he threatened.

Jack ignored the warning and thumbed through the papers, scanning each sheet. When he came to the last page he studied it thoroughly. A moment of dead silence passed slowly. He looked Marvin in the eye as he folded the papers. Suddenly he slapped him across the face with them.

"You stupid bastard!" His voice boomed angrily. "What kind of a bluff are you trying to pull on this woman? These papers are not even notarized. All you've got here is a legal form with a signature. Now, if you don't want me to beat the holy hell out of you, get out of here and don't come back."

"A mere technicality which I will remedy immediately. I'm not without influence in this state, as you'll soon discover." Marvin stuffed the papers in his pocket. "I'll be back with my attorney and the sheriff."

"Fine. If it's a fight for the boy you're wanting, I think we can give it to you."

Marvin opened his mouth as if to say something, but he changed his mind, and slowly pulled on his gloves instead. His face was unreadable as he turned and went out the door.

Jack stood at the door and watched him leave. Not a word was spoken until the long black car moved out of the drive and onto the highway. He turned to look at Gloria. Peter's arms were still locked about her neck.

"The papers are probably phony. Don't worry about it," he said lightly.

She shook her head. "No one has ever talked to him like that. He'll be back."

"Good. I hope he will, and I'll finish what I started."

"Oh, Jack! You shouldn't have interfered. He's very powerful. He won't rest until he's put you in jail!"

"Is . . . he gone?" Peter looked fearfully over his shoulder.

"Yup, he's gone. Come here, Bronco Billy. You're getting too big for your mother to hold."

"Do we have to go with . . . him?"

"Naw—who'd take care of Cisco and the cat?" Jack lifted him from Gloria's arms and set him on the floor. "You'd better find that cat before Cisco does. It'll take a while for them to get acquainted."

"You sent him away, didn't you, Jack? You didn't let him take us, did you?" Peter's eyes shone brightly through his tears. "Mom! Jack woulda hit him. I'll hit him, too, when I grow up."

"Hold on, Bronco. We'll have to talk about this hittin' business sometime."

"It's goin' to be all right, isn't it, Mom?" Peter looked up at her hopefully.

Gloria clamped her lips together and willed the tears to stay behind her eyelids. She nodded and tried to smile, silently saying, *I hope so, but don't count on it.*

"Sure it's goin' to be all right, Bronco. Now scoot and find that cat before he and Cisco tangle." Jack gave him a little push toward the door.

CHAPTER NINE

The clock on the shelf struck the quarter hour. The sound wafted into the small eternity of silence that followed Peter's happy shout at finding the kitten. Gloria had turned her back to Jack, not wanting him to see the tear-filled eyes she was dabbing with the balled tissue. When she felt his hands on her shoulders, she stiffened. She was deep in the pit of despair.

"Don't!"

"Look at me, Glory."

"You've really done it, now, Mr. Smart Guy. He'll come back with the sheriff and take Peter. Why couldn't you just stay out of it?" she added bitterly.

"It didn't occur to me that you'd give up without a fight."

She whirled. Her eyes blazed into his. "Fight? You don't fight a man as powerful as Marvin Masterson, especially if you're a *peon* like me! You run. If he catches up with you, you wait your chance and run again!" Rage, and a blinding headache, were making her sick to her stomach. "That's exactly what I'm going to do, and you'd better do the same or you'll find yourself in jail!" She brushed past him and headed for the room she shared with Peter.

Safely behind the closed door the tight reins she had held on her emotions broke, her face crumbled, and she burst into tears. Still crying she jerked open the dresser drawers and stuffed her clothes and Peter's into suitcases. When they were filled, she piled some things in the middle of a bedsheet and tied the corners together. She flung on her coat and pulled a stocking cap down over her ears. She didn't care that her face was tear streaked, or that her hair was hanging in strings about her face. All that mattered was to get away as fast as possible, and maybe, just maybe, Marvin wouldn't find her, and would give up and go back to Ohio.

Gloria threw open the door and ran straight into Jack. He put out his hands to steady her. "Ready? I was just coming to get you."

"Get your hands off me, you . . . bushman!" she snapped. "I don't need any help from you."

"Yes, you do. I'm all that's standing between you and that cold fish that's using Peter to get you back." His grip on her arms tightened.

She pushed at his chest. "Let me go! I don't want you to touch me ever again. I hate it!"

"You didn't hate it the other night."

Shame and anger seared through her. How could he be so vile as to remind her? Desperately and recklessly she tried to defend herself, but the words that fell from her lips came out in a torrent of lies and accusations that were uncharacteristic of her, words that she didn't really mean at all.

"You must admit there's quite a difference between you and Marvin. After *him,* I wanted to see what it

148

was like to have a real man! Can you blame me for taking advantage of your offer?"

"Shut up!" he snarled. His eyes darkened as his fingers hardened like steel bands about her arms. His face was like a stone statue, hard and bitter. Gloria was sure he was going to shake her. But instead his hands slipped around her throat and his mouth came down on hers savagely, relentlessly, prying her lips apart. His hands beneath her chin held her head immobile, and his mouth burned, delved, bruised.

He lifted his head, and she gasped for breath. Her heart was hammering so hard that her ears were ringing. She couldn't think. She couldn't speak. He stared down at her, and she shook her head in silent protest.

"Be my Glory of the other night," he whispered. She heard the words as if they were coming from a distance. She stood stock still, waiting for the dizziness to pass.

"No. . . ."

"You know there's something wonderful between us," he murmured. "I stayed away from you for a whole week to find out if what I felt for you was real and lasting. It is!" His mouth closed over hers as he kissed her gently. Her mouth trembled. "You see how it is with us?"

"No. I don't see that at all." She tried to twist away from him.

"Yes, you do. You're fighting it. You've totally disrupted my life and you're not going to scamper out of it like a pup with your tail between your legs until I'm sure it's what we both want."

"You have nothing to say about what I do! Now,

bug off! You're nothing to me, and . . . I despise everything about you . . . especially that beard!"

His bright-green eyes mocked her. "You're a liar, Glory, Glory," he drawled softly. "Not a word of what you've said is true, and you know it. You're hurt and miserable and frightened. I can understand that. But pretending that you hate me is juvenile."

She wanted so badly to hit him that her fists curled into tight balls. Only the fact that Peter was coming into the room stopped her.

"Mom! Mom! Are you coming? I got Cisco and the kitty in the car." Gloria felt the blast of cool air from the open door. "Jack said I could name the kitty, Mom. Jack said I ought to call her Lucy."

Jack's hands fell from her arms. "We're coming, Bronco Billy. Get back in the car." He stepped around Gloria and picked up the suitcases. "Is this all you're taking?"

"Yes. But I can manage by myself."

"I don't doubt that for a minute, but this time you're not going to. Leave it, I'll get it," he said when she attempted to intercept him. She could tell that he was angry, but his voice remained calm. He nudged her in the back to force her out the door ahead of him.

Janet was in the office. She looked anxiously at Gloria, and then followed her to the back door.

"Jack explained why you're leaving. That bastard! That no-good bum! Don't worry about the motel. Gary and I will be here."

"Tell Aunt Ethel I'll get in touch with her as soon as I can. Hey!" she yelled at Jack. "Don't put my things in that car."

"It's not a car, Mom. Jack said it's a Jeep. He said it

can go through snow." Peter's eyes danced with excitement as he climbed into the back of the vehicle.

Gloria fumed. *Jack said! Jack said!*

Jack lowered the back door of the Jeep and set the suitcases inside. He passed her without a glance and went back to the motel for the bundle. Gloria had the suitcases on the ground and was trying to get Peter out of the truck when Jack returned. Silently, and calmly, he put the suitcases back in, wedged the bundle between them, and slammed the door.

"Get in."

"No. I'm taking my own car. Peter, get out of—" Jack swung her up in his arms and sat her on the seat. "Now, wait just a doggone minute," she sputtered. "Who do you think—"

Peter shrieked with laughter. "Mom! Jack picked you up like he does me. Jack's stronger than anybody, Mom."

Jack grinned at her, slid in beside her, crowding her over to the passenger's side, and slammed the door. Before Gloria could find the door handle, the engine roared to life. He shifted the gears and backed the Jeep up so fast that Peter toppled over on the bundle, Cisco barked, and the frightened cat jumped over the seat and into Gloria's lap. They careened out onto the highway, Gloria grabbing the dash to keep from falling against Jack. She glanced at his face. His thick black hair was going in all directions, his eyes were mere slits, and his dark brows were drawn together. *He looks as fierce as a medieval warrior; all he needs is a suit of armor and a lance,* she thought.

"Where are you taking us?" she demanded. When

he ignored her she shouted the question, angrily, forgetting about Peter. "I said, where are you taking us?"

"To Hangtown."

If Jack had suddenly sprouted horns Gloria couldn't have been more shocked. For seconds she couldn't speak. Her heart fell right down through her stomach to her toes. It hadn't occurred to her that he would take them *there!*

"No way! We're going to Great Falls. I'll get a job—"

"Do you *want* him to find you?"

"You know I don't!"

"Can you think of a better place? The sheriff won't come out there; Hangtown is in another county. By the time he goes to Great Falls and gets a warrant, I'll have my lawyer in Chicago breathing down his neck."

"Your what?"

"Even bums like me have the right to legal counsel." He grinned at her.

Gloria snapped her teeth together in frustration, gave him a freezing look, and turned to gaze unseeingly out the window at the landscape that was flying by.

They turned off the highway and took a dirt road that wound among the foothills. Grass and weeds grew between the wheel tracks, and occasionally Jack had to slow the Jeep to a mere crawl. It was rugged, lonely country where stately cedars were scattered along the hillsides and gnarled oak clung to the ridges of an occasional arroyo. The Jeep rattled over a cattle guard and picked up speed, stirring the dry dirt into a cloud of red dust that floated along behind them like the tail of a giant kite.

The day was as dark and dreary as Gloria's mood. Gray clouds banked the northern sky, and the wind was damp and cold. Warm air from the heater blew on her legs and wafted up, making the inside of the car toasty warm. Gloria sat huddled in the corner, listening to the merry sound of her son playing with the puppy and the kitten. The dog barked, the kitten jumped up on Jack's shoulder, and Peter shrieked. Gloria couldn't even imagine Marvin in a situation such as this. She glanced at Jack. He didn't seem to even notice the confusion; in fact he seemed to be enjoying it.

When they reached Hangtown, Gloria understood what her aunt had meant when she said it was a ghost town. The main street wound steeply up a slope and ended abruptly at the bottom of a huge tailing dump below a gaping hole in the mountain and the relic of a mill that clung precariously to the side of it. Beyond that rose the shoulder of the mountain, its slopes covered with blue spruce, pine, and aspen. On each side of the street was a straggled line of old and weathered buildings; the roofs of some were caved in, their windows were mostly without glass, and their doors were missing or hanging by one hinge, making them look gaunt and cadaverous. An imposing false-fronted "saloon" sat on the corner and lorded it over the stores, which were all fronted by a sagging boardwalk. Some of the structures leaned one way, some another, some seemed in imminent danger of collapsing, and indeed several of those without stone foundations had.

"Welcome to Hangtown. The population is now four people, two dogs, six cats, and an ever-fluctuating number of wild animals."

"Who lives there?" she asked, pointing to the smoke curling upward from a cobblestone chimney at the end of the town.

"Another, slightly older hippy by the name of Cliff Rice. He's a part-time prospector."

Jack had stopped the Jeep in front of a building that had a new door and shiny new windows. The porch and steps had been replaced, but left unpainted. A CB antenna was attached to the side of the building and seemed to Gloria to be grossly out of place. She felt as if she had stepped back into time and that at any moment the saloon door would swing open and she would hear the tinkling sound of a piano. She looked down the dusty street, almost expecting to see a group of horsemen ride into town with blazing six-shooters.

Forgetting her earlier hostility she turned shining eyes to Jack. "It's right out of a John Wayne movie!"

"You like it?"

"Of course. I'm a western fan. I read every western novel I get my hands on."

He chuckled. "The ones, I suppose, where the hero and heroine ride off into the sunset and live happily ever after?"

"So? What's wrong with living happily ever after? When I finish a book I want to leave it with the feeling that all is right with the people I've met in the story. A bad ending leaves me depressed."

"You've got something there. If you want to feel depressed, you can read the newspaper."

"At least we agree about something."

"We agree about a lot of things, Glory, Glory. You just don't realize it yet." His hand reached out and gripped her shoulder. "You and Peter will stay here in

154

Hangtown until I find out which way the wind is blowing, okay?"

"Okay," she said reluctantly. "But it'll only delay the inevitable."

"Have a little faith in me, honey."

Peter jumped out of the car and the puppy followed. "I want to see your dog. I want to see Ringo."

"Hold it! Ringo's down with Cliff. We'd better leave him there until he gets acquainted with Cisco."

"Peter! Come back!" Gloria called anxiously.

"He'll be all right. He knows not to go into any of the buildings and to stay in sight. He's a smart boy."

She looked into his eyes and thought for the hundredth time that it should be a crime for a man to have such beautiful, expressive eyes. They were soft and moved lovingly over her face as his fingertips caressed her neck. *He fully intends to take advantage of the situation and seduce me into his bed again!* The bitter, shocking thought rocked her. Blood drained from her face, and her heartbeat slowed to a dull thud.

"I won't!"

"You won't what?"

"Sleep with you again!"

He laughed. "Want to bet on it?"

"You're conceited and crude!"

"Yeah, I am. Come to think about it, we didn't do much *sleeping* that night, did we?"

"You may think I'm old fashioned and super straight, but as I told you before, I don't sleep around."

"Thank God!"

"What does that mean?"

"It means that I'm glad you don't sleep around." His eyes were sparkling with laughter.

"Don't you dare laugh at me, you . . . you hairy ape!"

"If you're worried about your reputation, we can get married."

"That's very kind of you." She murmured softly, suddenly self-conscious. "Thank you very much, but I must decline your most generous offer to *save* my reputation."

"Good. I don't want you to marry me out of gratitude. I don't want you to marry me for any reason except the right one."

"And that is?" Her throat was tight, and the words were difficult to get out.

"Love, little sweet one. Love, spelled L-O-V-E. The only way I'll marry you is if you love me madly and want to live with me for the rest of your life, and because you want to share my dreams, my problems, raise my children, and be my companion as we grow old." His eyes raced over her and then rested on her trembling lips. She thought he was going to kiss her, and she moved back quickly.

"Is that all, Mr. Evans?"

"No, Glory, Glory. That isn't all. I want you to want me every night of my life as you did the other night. I want you to give yourself to me, laugh, play, break out of that shell you've built around yourself. I want to take care of you and Peter. I want to be the most important person in your lives."

"You think that covers all the bases, don't you? What about what *I* want?" The question was meant to sound menacing, as she tried to hide her confused thoughts behind anger. She felt as if she were floating away, losing control of her senses.

"What do you want, pretty girl?" He tugged at a strand of her hair and leaned close so he could look into her face.

Pride kept her rigid. "I *don't* want to raise my son in a hippie commune. I want more security for him than that! I want us to live a more structured life: steady income, a roof over our heads, a chance to make friends, plant roots somewhere. I want permanence."

"That's important to you, huh? You had all of that with the stuffed shirt." He yanked her to him, lowered his head, and kissed her softly, then more urgently. It took her breath from her. She struggled without success, and then finally surrendered to his superior strength. At last he lifted his head. His arms held her so tightly, she thought she would faint, and the blood pounded in her temples.

"You don't know what you want, Glory, Glory," he muttered. "I *know* that I want you in my life, in my bed, and . . . hell! I want you, period!" He grabbed her hand and held it against the aching hardness that throbbed between his legs. When she gasped and tried to pull her hand away, he tightened his grip on her wrist and held it there. "You've done that to me. You do it almost every time I'm with you. Dammit! Do you think I *want* to think of you every waking moment? I haven't had a peaceful moment since I met you. Sometimes I get so frustrated I could beat you!" She winced at the anger in his voice and tried to return his gaze coolly.

"Don't you threaten me, you . . . sex maniac!"

157

His scorching eyes ran over each feature of her face; then he laughed, a deep, rumbling, masculine laugh that boomed in her ears. He moved his face close to hers and tickled the end of her nose with his mustache. His eyes were sparkling green pools of amusement.

"Oh, Glory, you're a lot of things, but boring isn't one of them. You'd make a wonderful wife for a . . . sex maniac. It's almost as much fun to tease you as it is to make love to you. C'mon, honey. Melt a little and kiss me back."

Gloria squeezed her eyelids tightly together and tried desperately not to think about how warm and comforting it was to be in his arms. She fought the temptation to yield to the persuasive voice and gentle, coaxing lips. She was concentrating so hard that his hand moved under her jacket, and his long fingers delved beneath the waistband of her jeans and thin panties, and cupped the fullness of her rounded naked bottom before she came out of her trance.

"Stop that! Get your sneaky hand out of there!" she demanded. She pushed on his chest with all her strength. The arm across her shoulders tightened, the fingers in her jeans pinched her bottom. She let out a shriek. "Stop that!"

"Not until you kiss me." Laughter lines crinkled the corners of his eyes.

Gloria considered kicking him, but decided to capitulate due to his superior strength. She despised herself for doing it, but she forced herself to kiss him lightly on the lips, then moved her face as far back as his hold on her would allow.

"That won't do a-tall—not a-tall," he drawled. "Put your arms around my neck and kiss me like I know you can." His voice was a husky whisper, stirring little waves of response inside of her.

"What about Peter?"

"Happily playing on the porch," he murmured. His fingers caressed her flesh and traveled gently down the valley between her buttocks.

Gloria's arms moved up and around his neck, and she closed her eyes as she placed her mouth on his. A low triumphant sound came from his throat, crowing his power over her, but she didn't care anymore. When he lifted his lips to demand that she open her mouth, she unhesitantly obeyed. His tongue stroked her smooth, even lips, and the hand in her jeans caressed her bottom. Gloria felt a sudden rip in the fabric of her resentment that she had so tenuously wrapped around herself as protection from him. Swamped as she was by mounting desire, it became impossible for her to remain passive. Every cell in her body surged to life, blocking out everything except the touch of his mouth, the warm strength of his arms, and the gentle fingers inside her jeans.

A banging on the car door brought Gloria out of the haze and into the present. Her mind was foggy. Jack raised his mouth from hers and she looked over her shoulder to see Peter peering at them through the window. Jack reached across her lap and cranked down the window.

"How ya doin', Bronco?"

"What was you doing to Mom?"

"I was kissing her."

"Did she want you to?"

"Yeah—I think so."

Peter frowned. "Did you, Mom? Did you want Jack to kiss you?"

Gloria saw the worry on his small face. "Yes, I did. Grown-ups . . . ah . . . like to kiss . . . sometimes."

"You never kissed *him!* You like Jack, don't you, Mom?" Peter said hopefully. "You like him a lot?"

"Sure she does," Jack said, and the fingers in her jeans pinched gently.

"Okay . . . you can kiss her."

"Thanks, ol' man. We'll talk about this sometime, but now we'd better get inside and get you settled in before it gets dark. Get a hold on Cisco," Jack called, and reluctantly withdrew his hand from Gloria's naked flesh. He reached behind the seat for a leash and tossed it out to Peter. "Tie him up, Bronco. He doesn't know enough yet to stay away from a skunk." The arm around Gloria shook her gently in an attempt to make her look at him. She gazed out the window, and he spoke to her profile. "The sacrifices a man must make sometimes are enough to tear him up."

"Bull—"

"Don't be crude, sweetheart! Come on, shake a leg. If you're nice, I'll give you the fifty-cent tour of my home."

When Gloria stepped inside Jack's house, her first thought was that he had obviously put a lot of work into fixing it up. The long narrow main room was insulated and paneled. A big iron cookstove sat along side a white refrigerator-freezer. The room was sparsely furnished, but comfortable. A queen-size bed and bookshelves dominated the far end of the room.

The living space, kitchen, and sleeping area all flowed together and were amazingly neat.

"No electricity, so there's no TV," Jack said on his way to the back of the room with a suitcase under each arm. "Also, the bathroom is out back. There's hot water in the cookstove reservoir, if you can bathe in a washtub."

"If there's no electricity, how does the refrigerator work?"

"Bottled gas, sweetheart. We've also got a gaslight. By the way, back in the town's heyday, this building was the funeral parlor," he said gleefully as he went out the door.

"Wonderful," Gloria snapped over her shoulder. A small hand tugged at hers, and she looked down at her son.

"You like it here, don't you, Mom? Can we stay with Jack? You like him, don't you?"

The tight, worried, anxious little face pulled at her heartstrings. She knelt down beside him and folded him in her arms.

"Is that what you want to do, Peter?"

"I love Jack. He won't let *him* take us back."

"And I love you. We can't stay here forever, honey, but we'll stay a little while. Later on we must find us a place where I can get a job. Next year you'll be going to school." She tried to keep the anxiety out of her voice.

"Are we having a family conference?" Jack asked when he came in carrying the rest of the luggage. "If so, I want in on it."

"Mom says we'll stay here a little while, Jack. Then she's got to get a job in a town where I can go to school. When I grow up I'll get a job and take care of Mom."

Tears welled up in Gloria's eyes and she hugged her small son to her so he wouldn't see them, but she couldn't hide them from Jack.

"Ya just might have ta fight me fer the job, Bronco," Jack murmured in a staged voice. "C'mon, put up yer dukes!" He crouched and doubled up his fists. Shrieking with laughter Peter broke out of his mother's embrace. He knotted his small fists and began to pound Jack on the thigh. Jack groaned and doubled over as if in pain.

Gloria hastily wiped her tear-drenched eyes. Obviously Jack had played this game with her son before. With Jack, Peter was not at all quiet and withdrawn as he had been back in Ohio, where he had experienced Marvin's dislike. Now he was a personable, outgoing little boy, and Jack was responsible for the change. *Jack's enjoying himself, too,* Gloria thought. *He really and truly likes Peter!*

Jack lit the gas lamp and added more fuel to the cookstove. "When it gets really cold, I fire up the potbellied stove, too, and the two stoves keep this place surprisingly warm. But most of the time the cookstove is enough. How about ham and eggs for supper?"

"Fine. I'll fix it." Gloria dipped water from the reservoir and washed her hands in the granite washbowl. She could see Jack watching her. She'd show him that she wasn't helpless in these primitive surroundings. Her grandmother, on the farm in Ohio, had a woodburning cookstove. She'd spent summers with her while she was growing up. She'd learned how to build up the fire, shake down the ashes, and bank it for the night. "Move out of the way, I'll have supper ready in no time," she said, lifting the stove lid and setting an iron skillet directly over the flame.

"Hummm . . . hidden talents. This woman is keeping secrets from me." He watched her as she placed the slices of ham in the skillet. "Cook plenty, honey. I'm hungry as a bear." She raised her brows and looked pointedly at his beard. He laughed and scratched his chin. "You'd better get used to it, Glory. I'd sure hate to shave off these *glorious* whiskers. It's taken two years to grow them." When she didn't answer, he said, "No comment?"

"No comment."

"Okay. I'll leave it to you. I've got a bedroll and a camp cot in the back room. I'll make up a bed . . . for Peter," he added softly as he passed her.

Gloria's back stiffened, but she refused to rise to the bait.

CHAPTER TEN

In spite of the nagging feeling that she and Peter should not be here, that everything she'd ever believed in revolted at the thought of living in this primitive outback with a man like Jack Evans, Glory felt safe and peacefully content. She realized that if anyone could help her out of the predicament she was in, it was Jack.

After dinner she gave Peter a sponge bath, put him in his flannel pajamas, and tucked him in the big bed. He called for Jack to come and say good-night, then was almost instantly asleep.

Gloria was standing with her hands on her hips wondering how she was going to change her clothes, much less bathe herself, when she felt his hands on her shoulders. She jumped, and her frightened heart began to pound.

"Did I scare you?" Jack murmured.

"Don't sneak up on me like that."

He grinned. "I wasn't sneaking. You didn't hear me because your mind was far away. Peter is asleep."

"You must have worn him out today."

"Come sit down."

"I'm trying to figure out how I can hang a sheet in the corner so I'll have some privacy to bathe."

"Why? I've already seen all of you. Remember?"

"Yes!" she snapped. "And you're no gentleman to remind me!"

"I guess I'm no gentleman to ask you this either—but do you have to use the bathroom?" When she didn't answer, he laughed softly. "Embarrassed, sweetheart? Don't be. It's a natural function. I noticed you let Peter go outside the back door. Do you want me to get a chamberpot for him when I go to town?"

"No need. We'll only be here a day or two."

He took his jacket from the peg on the wall and draped it around her shoulders. He put a flashlight in her hand. "Come on. I'll point you in the right direction and wait in case you're attacked by a band of marauding Indians." The tone of his voice was light and teasing and intimate.

This is absolutely unreal, Gloria thought as he guided her to the door with an arm about her waist. Unreal as it was, she had never been as physically aware of a man as she was this big, gruff, hairy, sometimes aggravating man, who was so thoughtful of her and her son. Equally unreal was the overwhelming feeling of security she had when she was with him.

The new privy stood like a sentinel in the light from the sliver of moon coming up over the crest of the mountain. Gloria was not a stranger to outdoor toilets and realized this one had been constructed for comfort as well as for privacy and sanitation. She chuckled when she saw the reading material stacked neatly on the bench—*Sports Illustrated, Field and Stream, Playboy.* She'd have to bring out *Women's World,* she thought with a surpressed giggle. But on second thought it was too cold to linger longer than was absolutely necessary.

Jack was waiting for her on the path. "I'll go down and see old Cliff while you get ready for bed."

"It's awfully dark, isn't it?"

"Are you afraid?"

"No."

"Good girl. Will fifteen minutes give you enough time?"

"I suppose so. What about Peeping Toms? You don't have shades." He stood close to her and she had to tilt her head to look into his eyes.

"We usually have only four-legged Peeping Toms, but tonight there might be a two-legged one." He stuck out his tongue and began to pant and breathe heavily.

"Stop teasing, you . . . fathead!" Laughing, she turned the beam of the flashlight on his face in retaliation.

"Gimme that, you squirrely little screwball!" He put his arms around her and snatched the flashlight from her hand. Her low, soft laugh pleased every part of him. "I like to hear you laugh, Glory."

"Do you, now?" she murmured flippantly. "Here's your jacket. Get lost and don't come back for at least fifteen minutes."

She thrust the fleece-lined coat into his hands and stepped into the building. She closed the door, leaned her back against it, and wondered if she had lost her mind. Just being with him brought her pure, happy enjoyment. She *was* in love with this man; she was deeply, desperately, head over heels in love with this unconventional social outcast. She felt her heart leap, then settle into a pounding that left her breathless. Nothing good could come from loving such a man, her practical mind told her. But, oh, God, the gentle way he had kissed her! It couldn't have been a lie; he did care for her. She stood there for a long while trying to accept this totally impossible situation.

Gloria was in her long granny gown and woolly robe when Jack knocked on the back door. When he came in, he had a stack of firewood in his arms.

"It's going to get cold tonight." He knelt down in front of the cookstove and shoved in a few sticks of wood.

Gloria stared at his broad back, his shaggy dark hair. He was a sweet and gentle man, but he could be angry and violent too. What made him this way? she wondered. She searched her memory for a scrap of information about his past and realized that although she had been intimate with him, he had told her absolutely nothing about himself.

He stood up and closed the firebox door with his foot. "In the morning I'll start a fire in the heater and bring in enough wood to keep you warm all day. I told Cliff I'd be gone for a while tomorrow and for him to stick around."

"You're leaving us here alone?"

"Do you mind?"

"No. I'm surprised. I didn't think you'd bring us out here and leave us." Gloria turned to hide the disappointment on her face.

Jack walked over and stood beside her. "I'm not abandoning you and Peter. You're safe here. I'm going into town to make a few phone calls; I know a lawyer

167

in Chicago who can tell us what we're up against. Trust me, sweetheart. Masterson won't find you here, but if by some miracle he does, I'll not let him take you and Peter back to Ohio."

"He might find you."

"I hope so. It'll save me the trouble of looking for him."

"Oh, Jack—"

"Don't worry. Everything is going to be all right. I promise."

"I don't see how," she said grimly. "He *buys* everything! He'll file charges against you and have you put in jail!" Her face creased in worry lines, and she gripped his upper arms. "I don't want you to get in trouble on our account."

"Would it bother you if I was in trouble?" His voice was soft and his beautiful green eyes were achingly anxious. Gloria yearned to tell him it would devastate her if he was in trouble, but of course she couldn't do *that*.

"You know it would! You've been a good . . . friend."

"Friend?" The word came out slowly. "I want to be your friend, but I want to be your husband and your lover too." Her head was lowered, but the raw pain in his voice made her raise her eyes and look deeply into his. They stood for a long, silent moment, gazing at each other as if mesmerized, and then he said softly, "It's strange, Glory, I didn't think I was ready for a woman in my life. But I stayed away from you, and discovered I'm only half alive when I'm not with you."

Gloria's hands dropped from his arms and she

moved away from him. She stood with her back to him, her head bowed. *Oh, Lord,* she thought. *I don't want to hurt him! If I only had myself to consider, I'd live with him and take what happiness I could get. But I've got Peter. I want my son to know the security of belonging to a family, not to be attached to someone who would be here today and gone tomorrow. I can't tie myself to a man who is content to live a hand-to-mouth existence.*

"Please understand. I've got to think of Peter."

"It's a short life we live, Glory. How people feel about each other is much more important than money."

"I know that. Oh, how I know that. It's other things, Jack. Please don't talk about it."

He pulled her back against him. "When I'm near you, I can't keep my hands off you," he whispered in her ear. "It's more than wanting to take you to bed, it's wanting to hold you gently, take care of you, have you there when I wake in the morning, and all the rest of the day."

She turned and put her arms around his neck. "Oh, Jack, I don't want to hurt you. I don't know what I would have done without you these last few weeks. You've been so good to me and to Peter." She began to cry, silently, with tears streaming down her face.

"Sweetheart, don't cry. I know what's bothering you. You think I'm a lazy, shiftless bum, squatting on another man's property. You think I'm a social drop-out living on welfare, and you'd be ashamed to take me home to your folks." She buried her face against him and refused to look at him. He held her for a long while, stroking her back. "It's all right, my honey, my love." The words were torn from him in an agonized whisper.

"I owe you so much."

His hands on her back stopped for a minute. He took a deep breath. "Mention that again, dear heart, and I'll have to do one of two things—spank you, or kiss you. You *owe* me absolutely nothing." His voice was shaky and his breathing ragged in her ear. "Come sit with me and let me hold you."

Jack took the Indian blanket from the back of the big armchair, sat down, and drew her carefully down on his lap. He held her tightly to him and tucked the blanket around her. It was like holding a skinny little kitten, he thought, cuddling her close against his chest. His face was engulfed in the fragrance of her hair, and her body felt warm against his. He drew a very unsteady breath, his mind racing, thoughts of the past and the future tumbling over each other.

Glory, Glory, I was so sure that after I lost Wendy, I'd never love anything or anyone again. And here I am, desperately, hopelessly in love with you. I want you for my wife. I want to raise Peter as my son, I want us to be a family. I want! I want! His mind skidded in another direction and he thought with a sudden realization—*Evans, you bastard! You want it all without giving up a thing!*

An hour passed while his mind grappled with endless questions. He tilted his head so he could look into the face of the woman in his arms. She was asleep, and she was softly, sweetly, sublimely beautiful! He looked at her as if seeing her for the first time. He had never noticed the unbelievable delicacy of her face, her bones, her shell-pink ear, so perfectly formed. Her

170

pink lips were slightly parted and the breath that came from them was warm and moist; he fought the urge to kiss them lest he awaken her. She was a curious combination of innocence and sensuality which had become an obsession with him. He felt lightheaded with all the swelling and churning going on inside him.

Long past midnight Jack rose from the chair with Gloria in his arms and carried her to the big bed. He stood holding her for a long moment, reluctant to put her down. Then he gently placed her beside Peter and covered them. He turned off the light and went back to the chair. He had some heavy thinking to do before morning.

As soon as Gloria was awake, she knew that she and Peter were alone in the building. The room was filled with light. She sat up in bed and looked toward the front windows. There was snow on the roof of the building across the street. She slipped her bare feet into her slippers and picked up the robe that lay on the foot of the bed. While putting it on she crossed the room and peered out the window. A foot of snow covered the ground. The entire town looked fresh and clean.

She stared at the empty space in front of the building where Jack had left the Jeep last night. The fact that there were no tracks in the snow told her he must have left hours ago. Snow was still coming down in huge fluffy flakes. It seemed to her the whole world was white, silent, and eerie, and she and Peter were alone in the center of it.

A tight little core of misery, Gloria stood beside the window looking out on the vastness, her body erect,

171

her eyes wide and unseeing, her heart beating in painful bursts. Confused and terribly lonely she wondered how she would get through the day.

When Peter awakened he was disappointed to find that Jack had gone. He sulked through breakfast, but brightened with the promise that he could go out and play in the snow. It took ten minutes to get him into his snowsuit and boots and out the door; in another ten minutes, however, he was back inside. It wasn't much fun playing alone; Gloria understood. She let him sit at the table with a pencil and paper, but that didn't last long either.

"When's Jack coming back?" He asked for what seemed like the hundredth time.

"I don't know, honey. He'll be back sometime today. Why don't you play with the kitten?"

"Mom . . ."

"Sshhh! I hear something." Gloria went to the window and looked down the snow-covered street. The empty buildings stood gaunt and lonely, like silent sentinels, on either side of it. The sound that had alerted her was louder now; it reminded her of the buzz saw her grandfather had used on the farm in Ohio.

But it wasn't a buzz saw. Two squat, dark objects came skimming over the snow. Snowmobiles. They came into town from the far end, stirring up a fine flurry of snow in their wake. The dark-clad, helmeted figures looked as if they were from outer space. The machines came through town and stopped in front of the building where Jack lived as if they knew exactly where they were going.

Gloria darted back from the window. Fright set her heart pounding like a drum.

"Come here, Peter," she whispered. Frightened by the urgency in his mother's voice Peter ran to her. Gloria wrapped her arms around him and the two of them crouched in the corner beside the door.

"Be quiet, honey!"

"Who is it?"

"I don't know, but—" The sharp rap on the door cut off her words. She glanced quickly to assure herself that the bar was in place. The loud banging came again. Gloria's fear was slowly turning to panic. Marvin had sent someone to get her and Peter!

"He ain't here," the man on the porch yelled to his companion.

"There's a fire inside."

"Yeah, he probably built it up before he left. He'll be back. We might meet him on the road."

"How about the old man down at the other end?"

"He don't know nothin'. Let's go."

When the roar of the motors had faded in the distance, Gloria drew a deep breath and released Peter so he could go look out the window.

"They're gone, Mom. Why didn't we talk to them?"

Gloria didn't answer her son. She was more aware than ever that the drama with Marvin was still unfinished. She tried not to think about it, because to think about it made her feel hopelessly panicked.

Irrationally Gloria felt outraged at Jack. Jack had deserted her when she most needed him. Her anger soon threatened to give way to tears; she now realized how much she had grown to depend on him. She pulled herself together and took a roast from the

173

freezer; if she didn't keep busy she'd lose her mind, she thought as she worked with quick, jerky motions. A voice in her head berated her: *See what happens, you jerk, when you count on a man like Jack Evans? He takes you to the middle of nowhere and goes off and leaves you.*

Instantly she was ashamed, and she made herself breathe deeply to calm herself. "What if those men were thugs Marvin had sent to beat him up! Please, God, don't let them find him, don't let anything happen to him!" The thought haunted her mind.

It was the longest, most miserable day of Gloria's life. From the moment the men on the snowmobiles left town she had a sick, uneasy feeling in the pit of her stomach. At first she was angry because Jack had left her without saying where he was going or what he was going to do. Then, after thinking about it, she decided that Jack was a man who explained himself to no one. Life with him would be one crisis after another.

"But, oh, dear God," she muttered to herself. "I love him and I'd be far more unhappy without him than with him."

Jack looked out the window of the phone booth and watched the snowplow scraping the street while he listened to George Fisher, his lawyer and friend.

"If he's got a court order there isn't much you can do, Jack. I know the arrogant, puffed-up son of a bitch; he wants to be governor of Ohio so bad he can taste it. I'd run a bluff on him if I were you. You could tell him you'll take him to court for mentally abusing the child. The newspapers would love it."

"That's a good idea, George."

"Are you in love with the woman, Jack?"

"Absolutely."

"I'm glad for you. You've needed something stable in your life for a long time."

"By the way, I'm not coming back to Chicago. If you get a chance to sell the apartment houses, go ahead."

"It's been a good income. Are you sure you want out of the real estate business completely?"

"I'll keep Hangtown. Let the rest go, George. I want to try my hand at running a motel. A few years down the line I might even consider making Hangtown a tourist attraction."

"I don't doubt that you'd do it, if you set your mind to it. Okay, I'll put the apartments up for sale."

"I might have to get back to you about Masterson. He's not getting his hands on Gloria and Peter. If I can't run a bluff on him, I'll take him to court; then you might end up with the apartment houses."

"Just don't lose your temper and get arrested for assault and battery."

Jack laughed. "I'll give it a good try. Bye."

He turned up the collar of his coat, left the booth, and walked quickly down the street to the hotel. The black limousine in the parking lot could only belong to Masterson.

"What room is Masterson in?" he asked the desk clerk.

"Two oh three." The clerk looked up and stared at the big man in a fur-lined jacket with snowflakes on his thick, dark hair and beard. "But . . ."

"But what?" Jack's green eyes bored into the man's face.

"Nothing."

Jack didn't wait for the elevator. He took the stairs two at a time. He rapped on the door of room 203.

"Who is it?"

"Room service."

The door swung wide open and Jack was inside before Marvin could stop him. He sputtered and drew several deep breaths before he could regain his composure.

"Get out of here!"

"In a minute," Jack said evenly. "I want to make a few things clear to you."

"Get out, or I'll call the police."

"You try it, and I'll break your arm." Jack spoke softly, but he stared fixedly at Marvin.

"I've put in a call for the sheriff. He'll be here any moment."

"Then you'd better listen to what I have to say before he gets here. I just talked to my lawyer in Chicago, who, by the way, is a good friend of the chairman of the Republican party in your district."

"So what?" Marvin sneered. "I'm one of the largest contributors to the party."

"So this, you bastard!" Jack took a step forward and grabbed the front of Marvin's shirt. "If you make another move to force Gloria to come back to you, you'll find yourself in court on child abuse charges. Then the Republican party will dissociate themselves from you so fast it'll make your head swim, with or without your large donations."

"Why—why, I've never laid a hand on that kid!"

"There is such a thing as *mental* abuse, you know. That kid is scared to death of you! I wonder how the voters in your district would feel about a candidate who abused his wife *and* his child?"

Marvin's cheeks turned red. "I never abused her. I never even touched her after our wedding night."

Jack stood back and scratched his beard. "There's not a red-blooded man in your district who'd understand a man having a wife like Gloria and sleeping with her *one* time in five years. That would make mighty good copy for the tabloids."

"Damn you! I gave her everything."

"Everything but love and companionship."

"What can *you* give her? Look at you," Marvin sneered. "She wouldn't have been seen on the streets of Cincinnati talking to you."

"Maybe. Maybe not. But I've got a heart full of love for that woman, and, by God, you'd better leave her alone and flag your ass out of town while you've got one to flag. Gloria is through with you. Do I make myself clear? So get on the phone and call that judge, or I'm setting the wheels in motion that will ruin your political career whether a jury finds you guilty or not."

"It's blackmail!"

"Yeah."

Ten minutes later Jack left the room with the court order in his pocket and a smile on his face. He met the sheriff on the stairs and nodded a greeting as they passed.

CHAPTER ELEVEN

Afternoon turned into evening. Gloria fixed dinner for herself and Peter and made a pretense of eating with him. He was unusually quiet, and when she suggested he get ready for bed, he went willingly. She put him in the sleeping bag on the cot, and before she'd finished reading him a bedtime story, he was asleep. It was only seven o'clock, but to Gloria it seemed like the middle of the night.

She washed the dishes and put the roast in the warming oven of the cookstove. After that she filled the firebox and that of the potbellied stove with fuel Jack had left in the woodbox. She suddenly understood how the pioneer woman, alone with her children in an isolated cabin, must have felt as she waited for her man to come home from a dangerous mission. Almost without realizing it she went to Jack's old leather jacket hanging on a peg beside the door and buried her face in the soft lining. The familiar smell of his maleness brought a flood of tears to her eyes. She turned out the gas light, plunging the room into darkness, and took up vigil beside the window.

Minutes turned into hours. She became chilled, and reached for the jacket to drape about her shoulders.

She found herself obsessed with the memory of Jack's face, especially his beautiful green eyes. She had seen those eyes in so many different moods; they had laughed, teased, smiled, grown fierce with anger. She found she could not bear to think of them looking into hers with icy coolness in their depths, or into another woman's with warmth and love. She wondered if she would be able to bear the loneliness if she went away from him for good. *It's lonely now, knowing he'll be back,* she told herself, *but how would it be if I knew he'd never . . .* She shook her head, not wanting to think about it. She strained her eyes toward the horizon, watching and waiting for a moving speck, anything that would mean Jack was on his way home.

When she finally saw headlights in the darkness, she didn't know if she was sorry or glad; they could mean the two men were coming back, or they could mean Jack had returned. But soon she could see that it was one vehicle and not two separate ones. The lights came steadily forward, at times bright, at other times blurred, as the wheels stirred the light, fluffy snow.

When at last she could see the outline of the Jeep, such an overwhelming gush of relief swept over her that at first she felt weak and sagged against the window. By the time the Jeep had stopped in front of the building, new life had surged through her and she flung open the door and vaulted out onto the snow-covered porch.

"Jack!"

The lights and the motor were turned off and the door opened almost at the same time. Gloria jumped off the porch into knee-deep snow and struggled to reach the man getting out of the car.

"Jack! Oh, Jack—"

"Gloria, baby! What's wrong?" He came to meet her. She threw herself into his embrace. He clasped her to him, trying to hold her up out of the snow. Her arms were around him and her face pressed against his chest.

"I love you! Oh, I love you, Jack!" She sobbed. "I was so afraid they'd find you and hurt you. Don't leave me again!" Her arms tightened fiercely.

"It's all okay, baby. Everything's taken care of. Oh, my God! You'll freeze! You don't even have on a coat." He lifted her up in his arms and walked carefully, searching with his booted foot for the steps in the snow, then carried her into the building and kicked the door shut. "It's pitch-black in here."

"Did you hear what I said? I said, I love you." Gloria's voice was loud and insistent. "I want to live with you. I don't care if it's here . . . or in a shack . . . or on the road. . . . I'll get Peter to school somehow. Did you hear me, Jack?" she went on anxiously. "I love you . . . you idiot! Say something! Have you changed your mind about me?"

"Yes, I heard you, sweet and pretty girl. And I'll never hear words more beautiful," Jack said softly, and stood her on her feet. "And, no, I've not changed my mind about you. The day was a year long while I was trying to do what I had to do so I could get back to you." He wrapped her in his arms and strained her to him. "Say it again, sweetheart."

"I love you . . . Peter loves you. We need you," she whispered hoarsely, breathlessly.

"And I love you." He felt as if he would weep. "Oh,

sweetheart, we've got to get a light on and get you out of those wet jeans. Stay right here."

Jack found his way to the gaslight and lit it. Gloria blinked against the brightness, then her mouth dropped open as she gazed in stunned silence at the stranger looking back at her.

Handsome? No, beautiful. The curly dark hair was cut and styled to cover just the tops of his ears, and was lightly dusted with snow. His cheeks were flat, clean plains that sloped to a strong, square chin beneath his wide mouth. But for the moment his quizzical green eyes commanded all her attention; they were all that was familiar to her.

"Jack!" she moaned. "Say something so I'll know it's you."

"Glory, Glory, sweetheart—"

"You're a . . . stranger!"

"No. I'm the same. I'm the same on the inside."

"But . . . you loved the beard."

"I love you more."

"I don't know if . . . I like it."

He laughed, and the sound bounced into every corner of the room. "It'll take two years to grow another that long."

Gloria couldn't take her eyes off him. "It'll take some getting used to. Why did you do it?"

"I decided I couldn't face the next fifty years without you, and if you wanted a conventional husband, complete with clean-shaven face, three-piece suits and a briefcase, that's what you'd have—if I was lucky enough for you to accept me." The words fell from his lips softly and sincerely.

"I don't know what to say!" She ran to him and

threw herself in his arms. "I'm sorry, darling. I don't want you to change. I want you like you are." Slim arms wrapped themselves around his neck. He saw her lips trembling into the shape of syllables that were surely endearments, but her tears made them unintelligible, so that what reached his ears was the strangled rasping of a sob.

"Silly girl. I've not changed. What's on the outside of me doesn't change what's on the inside. I love you. I'll make a home for you and Peter wherever you want it to be."

He held her so tight she could scarcely breathe. She turned her face and nuzzled the warm flesh of his neck. The crackle of the fire was the only sound she heard above the beating of his heart. Her arms slid from his neck to wrap around his waist. She pressed her full length against him.

"Darling," he groaned huskily. "You're wreaking havoc with my self-control. If I start kissing you the way I want to kiss you, I'll not be able to stop. We've got to get you out of these wet clothes or you'll be sick."

She raised her head to look at him. He was so close, she could see every little detail of his face: the smoldering green eyes, the strong nose, the sensual curve of his mouth. She could smell the masculine smell of his body, and an aching stirred inside her. Then his lips were against hers, rough and demanding with an insistence that sent her blood thundering through her ears. His hands moved down her back, touching her hungrily, urgently. Naked desire left her trembling in his arms.

Jack was breathing heavily. He moved his lips from

hers and they traveled over her face and then, as if compelled, back to her mouth. He kissed her deeply.

"Glory, Glory . . ." He clasped her shoulders and pushed her from him. "Go get out of those wet clothes," he said almost crossly while his eyes lovingly devoured her.

She sat on his lap in the armchair beside the potbellied stove. The lamp was turned low, so that most of the room was in shadows. Gloria had put on her gown and robe, and Jack an old jogging suit and sheepskin slippers; the Indian blanket covered them. Her fingers moved gently over his face, tracing his lips, his brows. They were peacefully content to be together.

"I've got a lot to tell you," Jack murmured.

"I've something to tell you too. Two men were here today. I didn't go to the door."

"Good girl. In this case it would have been all right. I saw them down by Ethel's. They said they'd been here and there was a good plume of smoke coming out the chimney, so they knew someone was here. They're neighboring ranchers looking for a cat that's been bringing down their calves."

Gloria raised herself up so she could look at him. "I thought Marvin had sent them out here to hurt you."

"No, pretty girl. You can forget Marvin. I scared the pants off him. He'll not give you any more trouble."

"You what? Marvin isn't scared of anything. He'll hire thugs—"

"I scared him with the power of the press." Jack laughed at the puzzled look on her face and pressed her head to his shoulder. "I talked to a friend of mine

183

in Chicago and he suggested I run a bluff. But it really wasn't a bluff; I was prepared to drag him through the courts for mentally abusing that child. He's so set on a political career, he backed off and called the judge in Ohio and told him he was relinquishing custody rights and would allow me to adopt Peter. For the child's good, of course."

"Of course! Oh, Jack. Do you mean we don't have to worry about Marvin?"

"That's just what I mean, pretty girl." He kissed her lingeringly. "Glory, it's time I bared all the secrets of my sordid past, if you're going to share my future."

"I don't care about your past," Gloria said, suddenly frightened that what he would tell her would snatch away her happiness.

"I want to tell you . . . before I start making love to you. I may never stop." He punctuated the words with soft, loving kisses.

He proceeded to tell her about his marriage to his high-school sweetheart and how, because of their immaturity, the marriage had been doomed from the start. He told her about the divorce, and his wife's subsequent remarriage to a man with underworld connections that eventually led to her and his daughter's death.

"I felt I had failed Wendy. My spirits were at the lowest ebb of my life when I came here to Hangtown. My little girl had died in a faraway place. . . ." He paused and buried his face in her hair, then continued in a husky whisper. "I didn't care for anything or anybody. I was living in a kind of limbo until I met you and Peter. I kept thinking that if I could break out and reach you, I'd find peace."

"Oh, Jack! Oh, darling . . ." Gloria stroked his head. "And I was so nasty to you, so narrow minded!" Her face was against his, and she felt his wet lashes against her skin.

"She was just a little girl and she's gone." There was anguish in his voice.

Gloria cradled his head in her arms and kissed him on his brow. "No, darling. She isn't gone. She'll always be in your heart—as you'll be in mine."

"I fought back the only way I knew how—in the courts. I had a small real estate business and spent everything I made trying to get custody of Wendy. When it was over, I just drove out of town. I'd bought Hangtown several years before while I was out here on a hunting trip. So I came here and holed up, licking my wounds."

Gloria looked at him, her amber eyes filled with love. "I don't know that I would have done differently, under the same circumstances."

"I really am kind of a hippie, sweetheart. I own two apartment buildings in Chicago, and the rent money goes to pay the mortgages. There's a little left over, but not a lot. We can live here, and I'll get a job, or we can run Ethel's motel, and someday maybe turn this town into a tourist attraction. It's your choice."

"Are your intentions honorable, Mr. Evans?"

"Right at the moment? No way! Later, like tomorrow, we're jumping the broomstick together."

"Like the pioneers?"

"Like the pioneers."

"I've decided." She giggled happily. "We can run Aunt Ethel's motel for now—then, later, I want to live right here in Hangtown. After all, how many women have a town all to themselves?"

"You're sure?"

"I was never more sure of anything in my life. Oh, darling, I'm so glad Peter and I came out here." Gloria's eyes became misty. "Jack, my sweet, wonderful bear of a man! Thank you! Peter and I were so afraid we'd have to go back to Ohio."

"The only man you'll ever have to obey again is me," he growled, and began to kiss her. "Hummm . . . you taste so good." His hand moved up under her gown and stroked the naked flesh of her thigh and hips. "Can we go to bed now?"

"Jack, be good. It's almost like kissing a stranger. I miss your beard!"

"You miss my beard?" His head came up and laughing green eyes caught laughing amber ones. "Good God, woman! For weeks you've been telling me I looked like a hairy ape. It cost me thirty bucks to get my hair cut and styled and my beard shaved off. I did it to please you, and almost froze my face on the way home."

She let out a girlish little gurgle of laughter.

"Poor baby," she crooned tenderly. "You can grow it back." She pulled his head down to hers and kissed him firmly on the lips. "But forget the earring!"

"Is there no pleasing you, little squirrely worry-wart?" he demanded, pinching her bottom gently.

"Yes. Did you notice that Peter is sleeping on the cot?"

"You bet! It's the first thing I noticed when I turned on the light."

"Well . . . ?"

Jack laughed joyously and hugged her close. "There's more I want to tell you, and I'd better do it now. Once I get you in that bed, there'll be no more talking." He began to kiss her and nuzzle her cheek with his nose. "Someday when we've made our fortune, we'll build a house right here in Hangtown."

"You're going to open up the town?"

"We'll have to wait and see about that. This is our town. We'll populate it ourselves."

"Ahhh . . . nice. . . ." she breathed against his cheek. "Can we get started now?"

"You wouldn't mind living out here?"

"Not as long as you're here and we're working on our . . . project of . . . populating the town." She stroked the dark curls back from his forehead, loving the freedom to caress him. This precious intimacy was making her light-headed with happiness.

"Our house will have two stories and plenty of bedrooms for Peter and his brothers and sisters. One for Aunt Ethel, too, if she is able to come." His voice grew husky as his lips moved over her face, but he continued determinedly. "It'll have a high-pitched roof, gables, a big porch with gingerbread, and a chandelier from Austria—all straight out of the eighteen seventies. How does that sound?"

"Fine, but we've got to make our fortune first," she whispered, her lips taking up the kissing. "You can tell me about it tomorrow. Right now I'd rather find out what it's like to have a . . . sex maniac make love to me."

"You're not going to forget that, are you?" He laughed joyously and got to his feet with her in his arms.

"No. And I'm not going to let you forget it either. I hope we're snowed in for a week," she said saucily, her amber eyes sparkling. She placed a little string of kisses along his jaw, and her fingers burrowed beneath his shirt and pulled at a tuft of hair on his chest. "Ya think you're pretty tough, don'tcha, big man?"

"I'm tough enough to handle you, mama chick. I'm from the Big Windy."

"Yeah . . . yeah . . . play it again, Sam."

"You're cruisin' for a bruisin', babe."

He dropped her on the bed and stood over her. She looked up at him with adoration in her eyes, but her voice was mockingly stern.

"Well, get on with it, tough guy, or I'll . . . break your arm!"